GONE... BUT WHERE?

DI SARA RAMSEY
BOOK TWENTY-FOUR

M A COMLEY

For Mum, you never let me down, thank you for giving me the tools and the backing to begin this incredible journey. Thank you for always believing in me.

Miss you every minute of every day, you truly were a Mum in a million. My heart, my soul.

ACKNOWLEDGMENTS

Special thanks as always go to @studioenp for their superb cover design expertise.

My heartfelt thanks go to my wonderful editor Emmy, and my proofreaders Joseph and Barbara for spotting all the lingering nits.

Thank you also to my amazing ARC Group who help to keep me sane during this process.

To Mary, gone, but never forgotten. I hope you found the peace you were searching for my dear friend. I miss you each and every day.

ALSO BY M A COMLEY

Blind Justice (Novella)

Cruel Justice (Book #1)

Mortal Justice (Novella)

Impeding Justice (Book #2)

Final Justice (Book #3)

Foul Justice (Book #4)

Guaranteed Justice (Book #5)

Ultimate Justice (Book #6)

Virtual Justice (Book #7)

Hostile Justice (Book #8)

Tortured Justice (Book #9)

Rough Justice (Book #10)

Dubious Justice (Book #11)

Calculated Justice (Book #12)

Twisted Justice (Book #13)

Justice at Christmas (Short Story)

Prime Justice (Book #14)

Heroic Justice (Book #15)

Shameful Justice (Book #16)

Immoral Justice (Book #17)

Toxic Justice (Book #18)

Overdue Justice (Book #19)

Unfair Justice (a 10,000 word short story)

Irrational Justice (a 10,000 word short story)

Seeking Justice (a 15,000 word novella)

PROLOGUE

e took another peek at his watch, the fourth
time in the last fifty minutes. The final hour of
his working day had dragged beyond belief. MP Ray Todd
was at the end of his tether, a Conservative member for
twenty years and an MP for his constituency for almost
fifteen of those years. However, since the start of the
pandemic his heart was no longer in his job. The threats he'd
suffered recently had put paid to the joy he'd once had for his
role.

This evening had been the last straw. The final two
members of the public who had booked appointments to see
him at his surgery had verbally attacked him. Called him
dozens of repulsive names, some of which he hadn't even
recognised, but their meaning hadn't been lost on him, not
with the way the two men had sneered at him when they'd
used the derogatory terms to address him.

Both men, Sean Potts and Mike Wade, had been escorted
off the premises by the bodyguard Ray had needed to fork
out for from his own pocket, after two of his MP friends had
sadly lost their lives.

"There has got to be more to life than this, hasn't there?" he had whined over a coffee when his bodyguard had returned to the office.

"It's definitely getting worse, sir. I'm not sure what the answer is. People these days are so angry with life."

"With life or with politicians? I think the latter, which is why I'm considering jumping ship before it's too late."

Andy's eyes widened when he heard the news. "Really, you'd do that, sir? But I thought you enjoyed your role and what it entails."

"I used to, a long time ago. I'm struggling to deal with the anger and animosity I have to contend with during my weekly surgeries."

"I don't blame you, but what will you do instead?"

"I don't know, retire abroad sounds as good an option as any. We'll see. I might wake up tomorrow and totally think the opposite. Let's call it a day. Do you want to join me for a swift half across the road?"

Andy grinned. "You read my mind. The missus is out at bingo tonight, so I won't have her bending my ear if I arrive home late."

"Fortunately, I no longer have that problem, not since my wife died. Now Sophie, my fifteen-year-old daughter, going on thirty, is a different story entirely. She'll be at home with her head in her books, doing me proud, the way she always has."

"You're lucky. Most of my friends complain they have to read their kids the riot act before they knuckle down to their homework."

"I guess I am. Sophie's always had her head screwed on. I'm so delighted with the progress she has made this year. Not sure if she knows that or not, though."

"I'm sure she does."

Andy helped Ray lock up, then he checked the street

outside was clear of any riff-raff intent on making a show of themselves, and they headed over to The Fox And The Moon pub. Ray bought the first drink, and the second, to show his appreciation for Andy's prompt actions in escorting the two troublemakers from the office.

"Well, I'd better make a move before my daughter thinks I've deserted her. I think I'll stop off at the chip shop on the way home, I haven't treated her to a takeaway for a while. What are your plans for the rest of the evening, Andy?"

He shrugged. "I'm not sure. I'll have to see if Ellen has left me a to-do list propped up against the kettle when I get home, that's not unheard of. If I don't see one, then I'll probably put my feet up and catch up on the matches I missed over the weekend. At least I'll have some peace and quiet while I watch the goals go in."

Both men laughed and parted once they left the pub.

"My car is over on the right tonight. Take care, Andy."

"You, too, boss. Glad you're still taking my advice about altering where you park your motor every night."

"I always listen to your advice. Enjoy your footie."

Andy raised his thumb, pulled his collar around his neck to combat the gust of wind that had just struck up and headed off in the opposite direction.

Ray was in a world of his own as he crossed the road to his car. A blast of a horn soon made him pay attention to his surroundings. The car swerved just in time, and he held a hand up to acknowledge his mistake. The driver gave him the finger.

"Charming. Same to you, arsehole."

He reached his car, scanned the vicinity, ensuring there wasn't anyone lingering in the area, and jumped behind the steering wheel. His home was a ten-minute drive away, and the chip shop was just around the corner. He didn't bother calling Sophie because she always plumped for the same thing: battered sausage and a portion of curry sauce to accompany her chips. He decided on haddock and chips and scrolled through the news headlines on his phone while he waited for the fish to cook.

Ten minutes later and with the tempting aroma filling the car, he went home. Once he had arrived, he called Sophie to join him for a surprise, but the silence upstairs puzzled him. Removing his shoes at the front door, he made his way up the newly laid stair carpet, along the landing to his daughter's room, and knocked on the door.

"Soph, did you hear me? I stopped off at the chippy. Are you coming down to join me?"

The silence concerned him further. This was unlike her; she wasn't the type to ignore him. He took the plunge and eased the door open. Her bedroom was empty and the door to the en suite wide open.

"Sophie, are you in the loo?"

There was no joy in there either. He ran back downstairs and checked the lounge and the kitchen, to find them both empty. Hand shaking, he removed his phone from his pocket and dialled his daughter's number which was immediately diverted to her answerphone.

"Where the hell are you?"

Frantic, his mind going over different unthinkable scenarios, he checked every nook and cranny inside and outside the property just in case she was playing hide and seek with him. He called out her name every few seconds and, before long, his voice became hoarse out of frustration. Then he ran next door to his immediate neighbours who both had daughters Sophie's age, thinking she might have nipped over there to discuss an issue with her homework. But neither the parents nor Sophie's friends had seen her since they'd finished school.

Ray returned to his house, shoulders slumped, by now

imagining all sorts might have happened to his beautiful daughter. He pulled out a chair at the kitchen table and rang his parents. "Hello, Mum. I'm sorry I haven't been in touch lately. I was wondering if Sophie is with you."

"Ray, is that you? No, she isn't. We haven't seen her in months, not since you two walked out on us after the row you had with your father."

"I'm sorry to have troubled you." He was about to hang up when his mother's sobbing stopped him. "Mum, what is it?"

"I miss you both. Where is she? Are you telling me she's missing?"

"I don't know what to tell you, Mum. I'm trying not to think the worst right now, but that's getting more and more difficult to do. I came home late from work, expecting her to be here, but she's not."

"Have you rung her?"

"Of course I have," he snapped. "Sorry, I shouldn't be having a go at you. I've got to go. Will you ring me if she shows up there?"

"I will. Let me know if you find her, otherwise I'll be going out of my mind with worry. It was good speaking to you, son."

"I've got to go now, Mum. I'll ring you if I hear anything." He reluctantly hung up on her. He'd missed speaking to his mother, but that was down to his father's pig-headedness. Whenever he and Sophie visited his parents, his father always seemed to go for his jugular, talking politics when he and his mother had warned his father not to broach the subject because it invariably ended up in an argument.

Next, he rang his wife's mother. Judy was a regular visitor to the house. He'd made sure he stayed in touch with her after his wife had died, if only for Sophie's sake. She had become frail since her husband had passed away from liver cancer a couple of years ago. He hated worrying her like this, but he needed to know if she'd laid eyes on Sophie this evening or not.

"Hi, Judy, how are you?"

"Hello, stranger, I'm faring okay. How are you and Sophie getting along? I haven't seen either of you in a few months, and no, that's not a dig, I appreciate how busy you both are."

Ray sighed. Judy had unknowingly already given him the answer he was seeking. "We're fine. Sophie is out with friends at the moment. I thought I'd check in to see how you're getting on while I have a spare few minutes."

"How wonderful. I was thinking, maybe you'd both like to come to dinner on Sunday? We could have a proper catch-up then, couldn't we?"

"That's a date. I'll check with Sophie and get back to you soon. Take care, Judy."

"You, too, Ray. Enjoy the rest of your evening."

"I'll be sure to do that." He ended the call and placed his hands over his face. "My God, Sophie, where the hell are you?"

Kerry, where are you when I need you the most?

His sister had also recently died due to unexpected complications, whilst being operated on at the local hospital. It had devastated the whole family and put an extra strain on everyone, which had only added to the feud between him and his father. He was in the process of selling her house at the moment. They had found a buyer and were waiting for the sale to finalise. Another situation that had taken up a lot of his valuable time in the past few weeks, drawing him away from his daughter's needs.

Why, oh why had I agreed to take on the burden? I should have left it for Mum and Dad to sort out. I thought I was doing the right thing at the time.

"Sophie, where are you?" he shouted, sheer exhaustion overwhelming him.

CHAPTER 1

*M*ark was still a little niggly with Sara after his operation. Maybe he felt his masculinity had been compromised when he'd had one of his testicles removed. Sara wasn't sure what was running through her husband's head because he'd failed to confide in her. She was still walking on eggshells at home nearly a month later.

"I'll see you tonight." He kissed her on the lips and added, "I should be home the normal time unless something major crops up."

Sara inclined her head and replied, "You know what the consultant told you, that it was imperative you take things easy. You pushed yourself too hard last week, and you know what happened."

He stared at her, long and hard, and then shook his head. "It's my body. I know I'm well enough to cope with the extra hours now. Doctors don't know everything. People have different levels of fitness once they have been through surgery. I was reasonably fit before I had my operation which has helped speed up my recovery."

Sara knew when to back off. She smiled. "Have a good

day. Give me a call at lunchtime, if you get the chance, to let me know how you are."

"Sara," he warned. "What have I told you about mollycoddling me?"

She winced and held up her hands. "Oops, guilty as charged, Your Honour."

He laughed and left the kitchen of their relatively new house. Sara remained seated on the stool at the kitchen island, even though she was tempted to wave him off at the front door. Something was making her stomach churn this morning. She gulped down the rest of her coffee. Picked up her cat, Misty, for an extra cuddle, fed her, let her out for a final pee in their small garden, then got ready to leave the house.

She was halfway to the front door when Carla, her partner, rang. "Hey, you, this is unusual, you ringing me at this time of the morning. Anything wrong?"

In the distance there were raised voices.

"I came into work early, don't ask, and things are kicking off here. How long are you going to be?"

"Kicking off? Er... I'm on my way, I'll be about twenty minutes, unless I use my siren. Forget that, I'll see you in fifteen. Can you manage to keep the peace until then?"

"I doubt it, but I'm prepared to give it my best shot."

Sara ended the call and double-checked the back door was locked as Carla's call had interrupted her morning routine. Misty wound herself around her legs as she tried to search for her keys and phone.

"Hey, are you trying to trip me up, help me to break a leg, so that I will take time off work to stay home with you? I don't have time for this, Munchkin." She hurriedly picked up Misty again, planted a sloppy kiss on the top of her head and placed her back on the floor.

She left the house and jumped into the car but resisted

the temptation to switch on her siren until she was much closer to Hereford when she could see the volume of traffic built up ahead of her. The opposite lane was clear, so she whizzed past the cars heading into the city and turned left at the roundabout when she found a break in the two-lane traffic. She arrived at the station within the fifteen minutes, as predicted, and prepared herself for what lay ahead of her, if the raised voices she'd heard before were anything to go by.

The desk sergeant, Jeff Makepeace, seemed relieved to see her the second she set foot in the reception area. Carla's cheeks were tinged a beetroot colour, and she was trying to get the irate man, who was seated, to calm down.

He flew to his feet the moment he spotted Sara. "This woman will help me, if you two clowns refuse to do anything, won't you?"

Sara took a step backwards as he advanced, at speed, towards her. Carla tried her best to detain him, but he shrugged her arm off.

"What's going on here?" At first Sara had trouble recognising the man. He was dressed in a crinkled suit and sporting a few hours' growth on his chin. His eyes were puffy and red. Then it dawned on her who he was. *Shit, this isn't going to turn out well, not once he realises who I am.* "What can I do for you, sir?"

He came to a halt in front of her. His expression had changed from desperation to what appeared to be guarded, and he mumbled an expletive under his breath that she just managed to catch. "I… umm… I need help."

"Shall we take this somewhere a little less public?" Sara asked.

Carla sighed. "Which is what I was trying to do when you arrived, boss."

Sara smiled. "I'll handle this now, Sergeant. Did you have a room in mind?"

"Interview Room Two is currently available, if Mr Todd is willing to go with you," Carla replied.

Sara smiled at the fuming man standing mere inches from her and asked, "Are you, Mr Todd?"

"Only if you're prepared to take me seriously. If not, then I'd rather stay here and keep battling it out with you guys until you're prepared to listen to me."

"We can give it a try. Come this way. Can someone bring us in a couple of coffees? How do you prefer yours, Mr Todd?"

"Black will do fine, with two sugars to combat the shock."

Sara let the final part of his statement slide for now and requested that he accompany her down the hallway while Carla prepared their coffees. On their way to the interview room Sara practiced a new breathing exercise she'd discovered online to help her calm her nerves, aware that once Todd realised who she was he'd probably wipe the floor with her, like he had a few years back when she had first joined the Hereford station from Liverpool.

She opened the door and gestured for him to take a seat. He sat opposite her, his head bowed and his hands twisting nervously on the table in front of him.

Sara removed her notebook from her jacket pocket and flipped it open to a clean page. "Now, how can I help you here today?"

"My daughter has gone missing. I've been going out of my mind all night, praying that she would come home. She didn't."

"And your daughter is?"

"Sophie Todd, she's fifteen. A very bright girl who never does anything wrong, and before you ask, she's not into drugs or boys."

Sara glanced up from her notes and tilted her head. "Are you sure?"

"Yes, I'm positive. My daughter and I have a close relationship, she doesn't keep anything from me," he said, his words lacking any conviction.

The door opened, and Carla entered the room carrying a small tray on which there were three cups of coffee. She mouthed to Sara, asking her if she wanted her to stay. Sara nodded, and after distributing the coffees, Carla sat in the chair next to Sara.

"When was the last time you either saw or spoke to your daughter, Mr Todd?"

"Yesterday morning. I had to start work early. I woke her up at seven, as usual, told her I'd fixed her some breakfast and left the house."

"Did you actually see her?" Sara pushed.

"No. She was in the bathroom. She grunted at me through the door; she was cleaning her teeth at the time. I had an important meeting to get to and couldn't hang around, hence me setting up her breakfast for her."

"Which consisted of?"

"A bowl of granola. I poured enough milk in a jug and left it on the kitchen table, along with a glass of orange juice. It's her favourite breakfast."

"And was it still there when you got home?"

His eyes narrowed as he thought. "No, the table was clear, and the dishes and jug had been washed up and put away in the cupboards."

"I see. Are there just the two of you at home?"

He nodded. "My wife died when Sophie was only five. It's been me and her ever since, with a little help thrown into the mix from both sets of grandparents and my sister, until lately. She passed away about a month ago, complications with an operation she was having to her stomach."

"I'm sorry to hear that. How did your sister's death affect Sophie?"

"She's fifteen, how do you think it affected her?" he snapped back.

"Sorry, all I'm trying to do is get to Sophie's state of mind."

"She was over it. She always recovers quickly from the bad news that has blighted her life over the years."

"Does that include the death of her mother?" Sara asked.

"Yes. Is that it? Are you going to search for her now? We're wasting time, valuable time that could mean life or death."

Sara raised her pointed finger. "Life or death? What makes you believe she's in any danger?"

He released a huge sigh. "Jesus, now let me think about that for a moment... ah yes, because I'm a blasted MP."

His sarcasm wasn't lost on her. "I'm aware of that, sir. What I meant was, has anything happened lately that might lead you to be concerned for your daughter's welfare?"

"Plenty. Ask me another? I'm assuming that you're aware MPs are targeted daily by members of the public, mostly infuriated by our lack of action when dealing with their, often insignificant, problems or issues."

"I've read several reports about that being the case. However, the people who have been targeted are usually the MPs themselves, as opposed to members of their families. What makes you believe that someone has set out to target your daughter directly, instead of you?"

His eyes widened with anger. "It stands to reason, any idiot can see that, can't they?"

Sara cocked an eyebrow. "I'm sorry, I'm going to need more than that, sir. Has anyone in recent weeks or months gone out of their way to threaten either you or your family?"

He stood, tipping his chair over in the process. "Of course they have... well, not specifically come out and said it, but..."

"Do you have the names and addresses of these people?"

"Back at my office. Do you think one of them is guilty of kidnapping my daughter?"

Sara shrugged. "Isn't that what you're insinuating? That your daughter has been kidnapped rather than run away?"

"Yes, that's what I truly believe. There's no way she would have run away, she had no reason to do so, therefore she must have been kidnapped."

"We're going to need the names of the people you have received threats from and the dates any threats took place."

"I can't give them to you until I get to my surgery. I have several meetings lined up today. I need to go home and get cleaned up before I attend them. My objective coming here this morning was to ensure the police took my daughter's disappearance seriously."

"Which is what we're going to do, however, we won't be able to do that without you giving us certain information first."

"Shit, this is just delaying things further. I need you to get out there now and help me find her."

"And we will, but without the information we need from you first, that isn't going to happen, not unless you can remember the names of the people concerned so we can run them through the system."

He tugged at his hair as he ran his hands through it. "I can't remember them, not off the top of my head. I'd hate to give you false information at the beginning of the investigation. Are you telling me you're going to take my case on?"

"I'd like to help out, if I'm able to, but first..."

"I know, I know... you need that information. I'll go to my office now and get it for you. Don't let me down, Inspector. And in case you're wondering, I do recognise you and I'm willing to put the past behind us for the sake of my daughter. I was told earlier, by the sergeant manning the front desk, that you're the best officer this station has to offer. Let's hope you've improved since the last time we worked together, otherwise I will have no hesitation in making a complaint to your senior officer."

"As is your right, sir. I want to reassure you that I have no intention of letting either you or your daughter down, providing we have some genuine leads to go on first. As things stand, your daughter has been missing for less than twenty-four hours. We're going to need a list of her friends, information about the school she attends. What after-school clubs, if any, she is enrolled in. If she has a boyfriend, or if she is keen on a specific boy. And we're also going to need information about her family; we'll need to speak with both sets of grandparents, if they're still alive."

"They are. I spoke to my mother last night and also my wife's mother. They both said they hadn't seen her. I made out she was with a friend so I didn't worry them and that I'd forgotten about her being with that friend when I called. At least, I think I did. My mind is so confused right now."

"I understand. I want to assure you that you're in safe hands. My team and I will do our utmost to find out where your daughter is and why she has gone missing. Are you sure you've told us everything?"

"Yes, I've laid everything out on the table for you. What would I hope to achieve if I held back any information?"

What indeed. "Okay, then we'll wait to hear from you before we go any further. We'll need a photo of Sophie."

He nodded and scrolled through his mobile. "I'll send it to your phone."

"One last thing before you go."

Frowning, he faced them again. "And what's that?"

"I believe you should break the news to Sophie's grandparents."

"What? I can't do that, it'll make them sick with worry."

"That would be my advice, take it or leave it. I just think

your parents should be prepared in case Sophie either shows up at their homes or contacts them."

He held his clenched fist to his forehead and groaned. "Okay, I'll do it. But first I'll go to the office and collect the information you need. Do you want me to ring you? Or would you rather I drop it off at the station?"

Sara removed a business card from her pocket and left her seat. "You can ring me, if only to save time."

"I'll do that."

She and Carla escorted him back to the reception area. He left the station with a mumbled apology aimed at Carla and Jeff. Once the door to the main entrance closed, they all let out a relieved sigh.

"Jesus, it had to happen to him, didn't it?" Sara groaned and sank into the chair behind her.

"Why do you say that?" Carla asked. "I can't remember having the pleasure of his company before."

"I can," Jeff admitted. "I was at the demonstration as an extra resource. We were assigned to patrol the area outside Ray Todd's office. Things turned nasty quickly, I seem to remember."

Sara nodded. "They did. I think you were on holiday at the time, Carla. I showed up and tried to urge the crowd to back up; they were having none of it. The more I asked, the more they refused to cooperate. I told Todd to remain in his office until the demonstrators had moved on; he did the exact opposite. He came to his door after someone threw a brick through his office window and pulled me to one side. He was spitting feathers, told me to get the rabble back or he'd report me to the superintendent."

"What a bastard. So, what happened?" Carla asked.

"Jeff was the one who sorted it out. He knew a couple of the demonstrators and managed to talk them around. Thank God. Everything went back to normal quickly; within minutes, peace had descended. I tried to speak with Todd, get him to make a statement. He didn't want to know, told me he was too busy to deal with such rubbish and marched back into his office. Even though there had been criminal damage caused to his property, he didn't want the hassle of making a statement." Sara shrugged. "If that was how he wanted it, then fine, it suited me. Jeff and I instructed the officers attending the scene to return to their duties, and that was the last we heard of it, until a few weeks later when the Super had a word with me on the quiet."

Carla gasped. "What did he say?"

"He told me that Todd had slated me for the riot that had taken place. I think the Super was testing my resolve. I put him right, told him that it was a demonstration that had quickly got out of hand. Yes, there was criminal damage, but Todd refused to log a complaint. The Super said that he was aware how hot-headed Todd could be and basically told me that he wasn't prepared to take the discreet complaint Todd had made any further."

"That was magnanimous of him," Carla scoffed.

"I didn't make a big deal out of it because all I wanted to do was get on with my work and forget the incident ever happened. The Super praised the way I had solved a couple of recent cases and went on his way."

"Wow, that's amazing, and here we are, you the lead detective on his missing daughter's case."

"Yeah, don't remind me. I'm willing to forgive and forget, if he is. His daughter should be our priority, not what has gone on between us in the past."

Carla smiled. "That's all well and good to begin with, until the frustration kicks in and he decides to jump up and down on your bones."

Sara wagged her finger. "Oh, ye of little faith. It won't come to that. Not if I have my way."

"We'll see," Carla mumbled.

"I hope he wasn't too much bother for you, Jeff?" Sara rose from her seat.

"It was fortunate there were no members of the public in reception when he showed up. Not sure what I would have done with him if there had been."

"It's better not to think about it, Jeff. You know where I am if he comes by again and tries to cause trouble."

"I do, Inspector. Let's hope his daughter shows up soon. I dread to think what depths he'd be willing to sink to otherwise."

"We'll cross that bridge if, and when, we come to it. Let's make a start on her social media accounts, see what comes of them. See you later, Jeff. Oh, and can you sort out the house-to-house enquiries around Todd's property for me?"

"I'll do that now, ma'am."

Sara and Carla climbed the stairs to their main office.

"Hey, how come you're early?" Sara asked.

"My car is in for its yearly poke and stroke as Des likes to call it. He came with me and gave me a lift to work from the garage."

Sara laughed and shook her head. "I take it that means your MOT is due? I've never heard it called that before."

"Ah, but you knew what I meant, right?"

Sara switched on a few computer screens as she made her way to the drinks station. "I did. Coffee? Or is that a silly question?"

Carla held up a plastic water container. "I'm on a caffeine break. Des and I are on a health kick, and he's told me I should drink two litres of this stuff a day."

Sara raised an eyebrow. "Rather you than me. I'd have to be lost in the desert for three weeks before I took on that challenge."

17

"Without water at your disposal all that time, I believe you'd be dead."

Sara grinned. "Exactly." She shuddered. "I wouldn't be able to conceive what life without coffee would be like. So, you've woken up this morning and cut it out totally?"

Carla shrugged. "Yep. So far so good." She flipped the lid of the bottle and downed a huge swig.

Sara knew she should be encouraging her partner if she was on a new fitness regime, but she had her doubts about whether Carla would last long once the aroma of the coffee hit her with full force. "Wow, it's been all of what? A couple of hours?"

"Don't mock me. I'm determined to kick the caffeine into touch. Des says he thinks we'll be far more alert and have more energy overall."

"Well, who am I to argue with Des, if he's an expert in all things to do with Adam's ale?"

Carla sat behind her desk, hit a few keys on the computer, sat back and scrolled her finger over the mouse. "I've got her page up on Facebook. I'm just casting an eye through the last couple of months now, see if anything significant has happened and what her reaction has been."

"Great, I'll poke my head into my office, see what awaits me in there and be with you shortly. Saying that, you have my permission to interrupt my mundane chore at a moment's notice should anything meaty come up."

Sara left the door open, paused to take in the view of the Brecon Beacons, which were standing proud in the cloudless sunny sky, and then began to tackle the onerous task she loathed, sometimes with a passion. To her surprise, and gratitude, there were very few brown envelopes sitting in her in-tray this morning. She started up her computer to check if her emails made up for the lack of post. They didn't. There were only three that were marked 'urgent attention'. When she opened them, there was nothing urgent about the contents at all, not in her opinion. Nevertheless, she took a sip of her still piping-hot coffee and got her head down. The whole task took ten minutes in total, with a few shortcuts taken in between. She finished her drink and then rejoined her partner.

By this time, the rest of the team had arrived and were sitting at their desks.

"Morning, all. I assume Carla has brought you up to speed on the new case we've taken on this morning?"

The team all nodded.

"Jill, I'd like you to finish off the paperwork on the previous case before you lend a hand on this one. I had DCI Price breathing down my neck wanting the completed file yesterday. It was my intention to wrap it up today but, after what Carla and I were confronted with first thing, I believe my efforts are needed elsewhere."

"I've got this, don't worry, boss."

"I knew I'd be able to count on you. It shouldn't take you too long to dot the T's and cross the I's, or should that be the other way around?" Sara smirked.

Jill chuckled. "I get your drift."

Sara approached Carla's desk and asked, "Has anything showed up yet?"

Carla pointed at the screen. "She changed her profile pic to a photo of her aunt about a month ago, making her seem older than she is for anyone surfing the net."

"And you believe that might be a significant factor?"

"I'm not sure but I do believe it should be something worth our consideration."

"Okay, if that's what you think, we'll do it. What are her posts like? Upbeat or full of misery?"

"Hard to tell, I suppose a mixture of both really. They were all doom and gloom around the death of her aunt, but the more recent posts are somewhat... I'm grappling for the correct term to use."

"Try harder," Sara urged.

"I suppose I'd call them thoughtful, especially where a teenager is concerned. Some memes about losing a loved one. Others contemplating what's good about life. Nothing that I would necessarily be alarmed about that might lead me to be concerned about her mental health, if that makes sense?"

"It does. Which leads me to be optimistic about her disappearance."

Carla frowned and inclined her head. "Did you think she might have taken her own life?"

"I'm not sure, possibly. It was one of the grim thoughts that fleetingly passed through my mind. Okay, let's see what else we can find out about Sophie Todd, and quickly. I get the feeling that now Ray Todd has my personal number, he won't think twice about calling it several times a day."

"Bummer. I hope not, for your sake," Carla stated.

"It is what it is. He comes across as genuinely concerned about his daughter. Whether that's because there's more to this story than he's prepared to divulge at this early stage, well, only time will tell."

Right on cue, Sara's mobile rang. She crossed the room to answer it in private. "DI Sara Ramsey, how can I help?"

"It's Ray Todd, Inspector, we met earlier."

"Ah, yes, Mr Todd, I've been expecting your call."

"I have the two names for you, and the men's addresses."

"Great, you having their details will be a bonus for us. We'll make sure we visit them today."

"I was hoping you'd say that. Do you have a pen and paper handy?"

"Always. Fire away."

"The first is Sean Potts, he lives at fifty Meadowfield Gardens in Eign Hill. And the second is Mike Wade who lives close to the hospital. He's been on to me about the noise of the ambulances getting on his nerves. Or should I say, the sound of their sirens going off day and night during an emergency. His address is eighteen Unity Walk, do you know it?"

"I do, I believe it's the approach road to the hospital. Thanks for the useful information. How are you holding up? Or is that a daft question?"

"It is. Let's just say I'm better than I thought I would be, but that doesn't mean you can take your foot off the gas, Inspector. I'm desperate to find Sophie and I imagine, with your help, that will happen sooner rather than later."

"You can count on me and my team, we've already made a start."

"Oh, in what way? I thought you were waiting for me to get back to you with this information."

"We're never ones to sit around, not when time is of the essence, sir. We're delving into Sophie's social media accounts now. I should have asked, I presume she has a laptop at home?"

"She has."

"Do you remember seeing it in her room after she went missing?"

"It wasn't my main priority to look for it. I can go and check, it that'll help?"

"It would be good to know, thanks."

He took his mobile with him and tore up the stairs. "I'm in her bedroom now. She usually keeps it on the chest of drawers when it's not in use. It's not there."

"Can you hunt around, possibly nearer to the bed, underneath it perhaps, or possibly under the pillow?"

"Ah, yes, you're right, it's here, below her pillow."

"Does she have access to an iPad or maybe any other kind of tablet?"

"Yes, her grandmother bought her an iPad for Christmas last year. She uses it regularly, but I don't have a clue where she keeps it. Do you want me to call you back after I've had a hunt for it?"

"If you wouldn't mind. I'm going to get on the road now, but you can still ring me on this number. Good luck."

"Thank you, I think I'm going to need it. Her room is a typical teenager's, stuff everywhere. Nothing is ever where it should be." He ended the call.

"Charming, goodbye to you, too." She crossed the room to Carla's desk once more. "That was Todd. He's supplied me with the names of the two men we need to visit. Do you want to come with me, or shall I take Craig instead?"

Carla frowned. "Are you worried about your safety?"

"Not really. I suppose I'm erring on the side of caution. You seem to be involved in this task, it seems a shame to break your momentum."

"I'm easy. Whatever is best for you."

"I think it might be a good idea to have a male presence, in case either of the men kick off." Sara couldn't believe such words had tumbled out of her mouth. She'd never had any doubts about her partnership with Carla before, so why was she now finding this situation hard to get her head around?

A hurt expression swept over Carla's face but vanished as quickly as it had appeared. "It's your call. Let me know when you decide."

"I've decided, come on, let's go. I'll sign a Taser out and let Craig know where we are, just in case we need backup swiftly."

Carla had a brief word with Christine, who moved to sit at Carla's desk. "Christine's going to take over from me. Are you ready?"

"I'll fetch my jacket. Not that I think I'll need it in this weather, it's just more practical taking one with a weapon to hand."

"You don't have to make excuses to me. I'll bring my water with me, if that's okay?"

They left the station and jumped in the car.

"I owe you an apology," Sara said.

"Hey, what for?"

"For considering leaving you behind back there. I'm not sure what I was thinking. That thought has never crossed my mind before, and we've been involved in some pretty nasty cases together over the years."

"Well, I'm not one for pointing out your failings but…"

Sara laughed. "I just wanted to apologise and tell you it won't happen again. I'm not sure what got into me."

"Aren't you? I am. You're being extra cautious with this case because you know what the consequences are likely to be if you screw up."

"Maybe you're right. I never really gave it much thought. Will you accept my apology?"

"Of course, although there's no need for you to ever apologise. You're my boss, what you say goes, end of."

"Not at all. I can make mistakes just like any other copper employed at this station. I also want to give you my assurances that type of thing will never happen again."

"You're nuts and you're blowing it out of all proportion. Stop letting this man win, Sara."

"Is that what I'm doing? Allowing him to get under my skin at this early stage? I need to correct that."

"Yes, you do. You're an excellent police officer and you shouldn't allow Todd, or his tactless reputation, to cloud your judgement."

"You're right. I should listen to you more."

"You should, I always talk a lot of sense."

"Right, game on. Let's see if we can find Mike Wade first, he's the closest." She didn't need to put the address in the satnav because it was only five minutes up the road.

"What if he's not in?" Carla asked the one question that hadn't yet dawned on Sara.

"Then we'll ask his neighbours if they know where he works and visit him there. Why ask?"

"I don't know, it's usually something you class as a priority during an investigation."

"I get the feeling you're trying to catch me out."

Carla slapped a hand over her chest. "Me? Would I do such a thing?"

"You would."

A few minutes later they pulled up outside a small block of flats, only two storeys high. Every now and again the balconies were dotted with pot plants, brightening up the austere exterior.

"Right, brace yourself for what's to come."

"I'm fully braced. Don't forget to bring your Taser with you," Carla reminded her.

Sara removed the item from her glove box and, once they were out of the car, she slipped it into her jacket pocket. Her stomach whipped up a frenzy as they made their way up the steps to the second floor and along the concrete corridor to Wade's flat. She inhaled a breath to calm her nerves and knocked on the flaking painted front door.

A woman answered. She eyed them warily and pulled the door behind her, leaving it ajar. "Yes, do you want something?"

Sara and Carla both flashed their warrant cards, and the woman stared at them and shook her head.

"Fuck, what's he done now?"

"Is Mike in? We'd like a quick chat with him."

"Yes, he's sitting in his chair, as usual. Happy to slouch,

while I do everything that needs doing in the house. Men, lazy shits, most of them. Fuck knows why I got married a second time. I should have learnt my lesson after I kicked the first useless prick out."

Sara smiled. "Can we see him?"

The woman threw open the door and made a sweeping gesture for them to enter.

"Do you want us to remove our shoes?" Sara asked.

"No, you might want to wipe them on the way out, though," the woman quipped. "I'm Gina by the way."

"Thanks, Gina. Have you lived here long?"

"Too bloody long. I much prefer living out in the country, but no, Mike was adamant he wanted us to move to the town, and now he does nothing but complain about it. All day long. It's times like this I regret having perfect hearing. At least if I wore a hearing aid, I could switch the damn thing off once he got on his soapbox."

Sara grimaced. "Sorry to hear that. Is it certain things he likes to complain about?" She kept her voice low, barely above a whisper.

"You name it, he complains about it. From football to the cost-of-living crisis and anything and everything in between. No subject is off limits with my old man. Can I ask what he's done?"

"There's probably a connection with what you've already told us. We believe your husband visited MP Todd yesterday, at his surgery."

"Oh God, he threatened that he was going down there to have it out with him. Don't tell me he went ahead and did it?"

Sara nodded. "Is he through here?"

"Yes, sitting watching *Lorraine*, either that or *This Morning*. He's addicted to the bloody TV. Every day is the same. Nice to have the time to sit and put your feet up. I never seem to get the chance to do it. Do you want a cuppa?"

"No, we're fine. Don't worry about us."

"Go in. I'll be in the kitchen; I want nothing to do with this." She slammed the front door. "Mike, the cops are here to see you. Any trouble, you can take it outside. I've mopped through already this morning, I have no intention of doing it again." Then Gina slipped into the kitchen.

Sara rolled her eyes at Carla. "Ah, married bliss, don't you just love it?"

Carla stifled a giggle, and they entered the lounge. There, sitting in a comfy leather chair in a reclined position, was a man in his fifties. He had a can of beer resting on his over-sized stomach and a large bag of crisps he was munching on.

"Mr Wade? I'm DI Sara Ramsey, and this is my partner, DS Carla Jameson. We'd like to ask you a few questions if that's okay? Any chance of you switching off the TV?"

"Nope. Ask away. What brings you to my flat?"

Sara repositioned herself to stand between the man and his obsession.

"Hey, get out of the way, I was watching that. You can't come in here and do what you want. I know my rights."

"Are you going to give us your full attention?"

"I doubt it. I don't even give the wife that."

"I heard that," Gina shouted from the kitchen. "The sooner you answer their questions, the sooner they'll be out of your hair."

He listened to his wife, which was a huge surprise to Sara, and switched off the TV. He then pulled the lever on the side of his chair, and it propelled him upright.

"Go on then, what's this all about?"

"Thank you. We won't keep you too long, Mike. Where were you yesterday?"

"Here, for most of the day, why? Has someone been telling tales about me?"

"Not exactly. All day?"

"Is there something wrong with your ears? I said most of the day."

"Where did you go?"

"To the bookies to pick up some winnings they owed me."

Sara cocked her head. "Anywhere else?"

"Yeah, I went to see our local MP. That's shocked you, ain't it? Someone like me mixing with toffs like that."

"Not at all. That's what our MPs are there for. May I ask what your meeting was about?"

"You can. I wanted to ask him what he intends to do about the noise coming from the bloody hospital, especially those ambulances screaming past our house at all hours of the day and night. It's beyond a frigging joke, I can tell you."

"During your meeting with Mr Todd, did you get angry at all?" Sara folded her arms after she'd asked her question.

"Of course I did, it's hard not to when you get bastards like that treating you like you're nothing more than shit on their expensive shoes."

"Really? And did you leave the meeting satisfied with Mr Todd's answers?"

"Hardly. Next question. Hang on a minute, what's this all about? Then pray tell me why you're here? And why are you interrogating me about that jumped-up tosser?"

"That's not a very pleasant way to talk about a member of Parliament."

"Tough. He's useless, all friggin' politicians are if you want my opinion."

"I'm not sure it's appropriate. When you left Mr Todd's office, what time was it?"

"Around four-thirty. Next, you'll be asking me where I went afterwards, am I right?"

Sara smiled. "And where did you go?"

"To the pub up the road. My old mate, Sid, will vouch for me, he's in there every night around that time."

"I'll be sure to do that."

"What's he supposed to have done?" Gina asked from the doorway.

"Nothing, as far as we know. At this stage we're just making enquiries," Sara countered.

Gina's eyes formed tiny slits. "That ain't gonna wash with me, Inspector. You've come here for a reason, to specifically ask my husband about his visit to see the MP, why? I'm going to ask the most obvious question running through my mind: has something happened to him?"

Sara unfolded her arms and faced Gina. "No, Mr Todd is okay, but his daughter has gone missing."

Mike shot out of his chair and got in Sara's face. He prodded at his chest. "What the fuck? And you thought I was behind her disappearance? Are you fucking mad?" He raised his hands and clenched his fists until his arms shook and his face contorted with rage.

Gina ran towards him. Grabbed his fists and steered him back to his seat. "Sit down before you rupture a blood vessel, you stupid old fool."

His body trembled, and his head wobbled while his fury increased.

"What's going on here?" Sara asked, concerned.

"His temper gets the better of him at times. You'll have to forgive him, he's on blood pressure tablets, but it doesn't prevent him getting like this."

"A temper, you say? And what would have happened if you hadn't been in the room with us, Gina?"

"Nothing. He's too much of a coward to act upon any threats he makes. All talk and no trousers, as my old mum used to say."

"Did you get like this when you visited Mr Todd yesterday?"

"No. I swear I didn't. I said what I had to say to him and

walked away. And if he has told you anything different to that, he's a liar."

"What time did you get home from the pub?" Sara's gut instinct prodded her into thinking he was telling her the truth.

"Am I allowed to answer that question?" Gina asked.

Sara smiled and nodded. "You can."

"Ted had to help him home because he'd had a skinful, not that we can afford it. He walked in as *Coronation Street* was finishing. That would be at nine o'clock."

"Thank you, that's helpful. We'll check out your husband's alibi with the landlord," Sara replied.

"Do that, because I was definitely there. I can't believe you'd even think that I could be guilty of harming anyone. Yes, I might have a temper on me, but that doesn't mean I go around lumping seven bells out of anyone, or worse still, consider harming a member of their family. I've got daughters of my own, and the thought of one of them getting hurt makes me sick to my stomach, it does."

"I think we've heard enough. Thanks for your time."

Gina walked them back to the front door. "What happens now?"

"Providing your husband's alibi checks out, we won't be taking his involvement any further."

"Phew, that's a relief. He's all mouth, I promise you. I'm the one who is likely to harm someone when pushed. I mean... I'd have no hesitation in bopping somebody on the nose, if I was pushed hard enough."

Sara leaned in close and whispered, "I'll let you in on a secret, I'd do exactly the same as you. Take care, we'll be in touch if we have any further questions for either of you." She plucked a card from her pocket. "And if you think of anything I should know, please ring me on that number."

"I will. You have my word."

They left the house and walked back to the car.

"What are you thinking on this one?" Carla asked just before they got in.

Inside the car, Sara placed her Taser in the glove box again and sighed. "I don't think he's capable of kidnapping or harming anyone, let alone a teenage girl whose father happens to piss him off. You?"

"The same. I don't think he's got it in him physically, and that's not being unkind either."

"Yeah, I'm inclined to agree with you. I don't think I'll bother checking out his alibi, or would that be deemed as foolish of me?"

"Hmm... I'd cover my arse by sending uniform out to check. But I agree with you, the bloke just hasn't got it in him. Not that I would have the audacity to say that to his face."

They both laughed, and Sara input the next address in the satnav.

"Let's see what Sean Potts has to say."

WHEN THEY ARRIVED, Sean Potts was still in bed, and to say he wasn't best pleased to see them would be an understatement.

"You can't come in here accusing me of getting up to all sorts, I'm not a well man. My doctor has signed me off work for the last couple of months because I'm incapable of functioning correctly at work after losing my beloved wife, and here you are, accusing me of getting up to no good. Poor Sharon would be turning in her grave, if she had one. She hasn't, her wish was to be cremated. I've yet to get her ashes back from the funeral home."

Sara raised her hands. "There's no need for you to get

upset about this, Mr Potts, it's simply a line of enquiry we're investigating."

"Isn't there? I pay my MP a visit about a gripe I've got, and he dobs me in to the police. What's that all about? Am I not entitled to go and see him when he has a surgery on or what? I thought that was the whole idea of him opening his office up to the public." He scratched the stubble on his double chin.

"It is. Can you tell us what your gripe was about?"

"The binmen leaving more rubbish on this road than they pick up every time they come round here. It's happening more and more, and it's the kind folks, living on this street, my neighbours, who are out there putting things right after they drive off in a rush to get to the next patch. It's disgusting, the amount of litter that never makes it to their lorry. That can't be right, can it? I'm telling you, it's not. My neighbours have had enough of this shit. We all got together, and I took down a signed petition for him to do something about it. And do you know what the cheeky bastard told me to do with my petition?"

"No, but I can imagine."

"Oh no, it's not the obvious. If he'd told me where to shove it, I would have rammed it up his arse, not mine. No, he told me to get in touch with the council and make a formal complaint. Like that's going to make a sodding difference. The folks down there don't listen to the likes of us, despite charging us the earth for them to collect the rubbish in the first place. Christ, it's unbelievable what we get charged for our Council Tax compared to those living in London. I read the other week that Buck Palace only have to pay eighteen hundred pounds... Jesus, how is that fair, for the size of that place? Mine is getting on for three grand a year, for a three-bed. Where's the justice in that then? I was outraged and I think I had a right to be."

31

"Did you cause problems for Mr Todd?"

His gaze dropped to the carpet in the living room where they were sitting. "I flung the chair I was using to the other side of the room to make my point. Told him he was no better than the robbing buggers on the council and that he should be doing better for the public."

"And what happened then? How did Mr Todd react to your outburst?"

"I'll tell you what he did… he called out to that thug of his, and the brute escorted me off the premises. I was told never to return again, as if I were a bloody nobody. What's the point in him holding these surgeries when he's not prepared to listen to people who have genuine grievances? Here, I'll show you why I got so worked up about it." He picked up his mobile from the table and scrolled through his photos. "I took a video of me and my neighbours collecting all the debris the binmen had left behind. I'm not talking about a few pieces of crap here and there. Here, see for yourself."

He handed Sara his phone, and she watched Potts and five other people of a similar age bagging up cartons and tins that were littering the road. Some of the bins had been carelessly left on their sides instead of being stood upright.

"I'm sorry you had to deal with this issue. I can understand how upsetting it must be for you and the other residents."

"No you can't. This isn't a one-off. It happens every couple of weeks, and do you know what makes it worse?"

"No, but I'm sure you're going to tell me."

"Those idiots, the binmen, laugh when they drive off. Yes, a few of us have complained to the men, but it doesn't make a jot of difference. If anything, it's probably why they intentionally leave our road in a mess."

"It's appalling. Hey, if you've got the footage, I'd take it down to the town hall and demand to see the mayor, see what he makes of it. You just need to speak to the right person about your complaint."

"I thought I was by going to see our MP. He couldn't give two hoots about it, wouldn't even look at the video when I showed it to him. That's what pushed me over the edge, what really pissed me off."

"That would make me angry, too. I understand your grievances."

"And yet it's my house the police are sitting in. You've seen the proof, it's the binmen you should be hounding, not me. I've got a right to complain if I think a council worker isn't doing his job right, haven't I?"

"You have, that's correct. I wouldn't do this for everyone, but if you send me a clip of the video, I'll have a word with my friend who works for the council. He'd get it sorted for you." She gave him a business card with her email address.

"You'd do that for me? Despite coming here to give me a bollocking?"

Sara grinned. "That's not why we're here. We are aware there was a disturbance at the MP's office last night and we're trying to get to the bottom of it."

"I've told you all there is to tell you. That man's goon threw me out on my ear, and I walked home with my tail between my legs. There's nothing else to tell. Is that what your job consists of these days? Chasing up complaints made by our local MP?"

"There's more to it than that, I'm afraid. I can't really go into detail at this stage."

His brow twisted. "What's that supposed to mean? Are you telling me you've come around here to scare the shit out of me and aren't prepared to tell me why?"

"All we're doing is following up on a complaint that was made by the MP. Can I ask what time you arrived at his surgery?"

"Around five-thirty. He kept glancing at his watch throughout the meeting. I got the impression that he was keen to be somewhere else. It's not good, treating a member of your constituency like that, is it?"

"No, I agree. Where did you go after leaving his office?"

"I came straight home. No, I didn't. Tell a lie, I stopped off at the chip shop up the road, fancied fish and chips for my tea. Don't tell me you're going to say there's a law against having a takeaway nowadays? Although I have to agree, their prices are criminal compared to when I was a nipper. Back then we only had them on special occasions when I was a lad."

"Me, too. No, there's no crime involved with having a takeaway, sir. Okay, we'll leave you to it. Sorry to have disturbed you this morning. Don't forget to send me that video."

"I won't. I apologise for being a grouch when you first showed up, it was the frustration talking."

"All is forgotten. Take care, I'll get my friend to get in touch with you soon."

"That's kind. Thank you."

Sara left the house feeling deflated. It wasn't until they were near the car that she voiced her opinion to her partner. "I don't think he's capable of kidnapping Todd's daughter either, do you?"

"Nope, it takes a special kind of nutjob to become a kidnapper, as we know. Neither of the two men fits the profile, not in my mind."

"I agree. I suppose our next step should be to visit the school, see if they can come up with anything."

CHAPTER 2

*M*rs Cooke, the headmistress of St Matthew's
School in Holme Lacy, appeared upset to see
them. She clarified her demeanour during their conversation. "I'm sorry, but I'm struggling to get my head around the
fact that Sophie has gone missing. She's one of our brightest
students, or she used to be. I believe her grades began to
suffer not long after her aunt died. I called her to my office
about a month ago to see if there was anything I could do to
help her deal with her grief."

"And what was the outcome of that conversation?" Sara
asked.

"She told me she was working her way through the
grieving process and didn't want or feel the need to seek any
outside help. She insisted that if she could cope with her
mother's death at the age of five, it wouldn't take her long to
get over her aunt's death. All she needed was to be given the
time and understanding after suffering a tragic loss. I was
prepared to give her that, as were her teachers. Things
improved for a little while, but in the last couple of weeks
she'd reverted to being trapped in her shell again."

"So there was a problem, a serious one? Do you think it might have been more than the grief at play?"

Mrs Cooke shrugged. "Who knows? These days teenagers appear to carry the weight of the world on their fragile shoulders compared to when we were growing up. I try to reassure them that my door is always open, that all they need to do is confide in either me or a member of my staff, and their problems could be halved overnight."

"And you truly believe that?"

"Yes, I believe having an open discussion is a key element to understanding what is going on with teenagers today."

"Can you tell me what she was like in school yesterday? I take it she showed up for her lessons?"

"She did. Again, Mr Baldwin told me she was a bit reserved during his English lesson. The pupils took it in turns reading aloud, but she refused to, said she couldn't be bothered to read Shakespeare and that the school needed to move with the times. That came as a shock to me when Mr Baldwin told me. It's not just our school reading Shakespeare, it's part of the curriculum the Department of Education insist upon. All we're doing is abiding by the governing body's rules. The fact that I agree with her really doesn't come into it."

"Was Sophie nasty, or did she come right out and tell Mr Baldwin that she refused to read Shakespeare any more?"

"She was outspoken. I wouldn't say that she was necessarily rude, but her behaviour sparked a mini riot in the classroom, which left Mr Baldwin pulling his hair out. He's a stickler for carrying out his lessons by the book."

"Does she have many friends at school?"

"Not really, she's always been a popular girl but also liked to spend time on her own. The other pupils rallied around her once her aunt died. When the news broke this morning, I mean when Mr Todd rang me to tell me his daughter had gone missing, I immediately went to her class to see if any of her friends had heard from her. They all seemed to be as shellshocked as me about her disappearance."

"It's still early days yet, but we're hopeful that Sophie will be found soon. Will you allow us to speak to a few of the pupils who are considered close to her?"

"Of course. I think it would be remiss of me not to allow you to talk to them. I can arrange that for you now, if you like?"

"That would be great, thank you."

Mrs Cooke made the call and asked her secretary to find a room suitable for Sara and Carla to carry out the interviews. She hung up. "Can I arrange for some refreshments to be brought to you?"

"No, we're fine, but thank you for offering," Sara replied.

Mrs Cooke led them out of the office. "Have you managed to find a suitable room yet, Erin?"

The secretary nodded. "Yes, the second room on the right, Mrs Cooke. Amy and Nadine will be with you shortly."

"Excellent news. I'll show the detectives to the room, I shouldn't be long. When I get back, can you get Mr Smithfield on the phone for me. He rang me earlier, seeking some information about his son's grades. I said I would call him back once I had sourced them."

"I've got his number here," Erin replied.

Mrs Cooke showed them down the corridor to a small room off to the right. She switched on the light. "It's not used often, only when members of staff feel the need to give a pupil extra tuition or a reprimand. Thankfully, the latter is a rare occurrence. Please, make yourselves comfortable. I need to get back to my office. I have a busy agenda to look forward to today."

"Don't let us hold you up. All right if we put a chair outside the room? We'd prefer to interview the girls separately. There's more chance of getting to the nitty-gritty if we do that."

"Of course. Here, I'll take one with me." Mrs Cooke collected the nearby chair and excused herself from the room.

Sara arranged three chairs around one of the oblong Formica tables, and they settled into their seats until the pupils arrived. A slight knock, barely audible, interrupted their conversation. Sara leapt to her feet. She opened the door to find two teenage girls, one with long wavy brown hair and the other with short blonde hair tucked behind her ears.

"Hi, you must be Amy and Nadine. I'm DI Sara Ramsey, and this is my partner, DS Carla Jameson. We'd like to see you both separately, if that's okay?"

"Who do you want to see first?" the girl with the long brown hair asked.

"Why don't we start with you? And you are?"

"I'm Nadine."

The girls smiled at each other. Sara noted it was a cautious smile, instead of a beaming, reassuring one.

"If you'd like to take a seat, Amy, we'll be with you shortly."

Amy plonked herself down on the chair and withdrew her mobile from her pocket. Sara closed the door and sat opposite Nadine, who had already taken her seat.

"We'll try not to keep you too long. Are you aware why we've asked to see you today?"

"Yes, it's pretty obvious, considering our friend Sophie is missing. Do you know what's happened to her yet?"

"Not yet. When did you learn of her disappearance?"

"I had a suspicion something was going on last night when her dad rang me. It was past nine, and he wondered if I had seen her."

"And had you?"

"Not since we parted at the school gates. My mum was picking me up to take me to the dentist, which is about twenty miles away. It's the only one she trusts in the area. She used to live there before moving to Hereford when we were younger."

"And where is that?"

"Sorry, in Ledbury."

"Does Sophie confide in you? Tell you everything that goes on in her life?" Sara asked.

Nadine fidgeted in her chair and swept a clump of hair over her left shoulder. "I don't understand. We're very close, if that's what you're asking."

"I was. Does that mean she tells you everything that is going on or not?"

Nadine shrugged and mumbled, "I suppose so. But if you're asking me if she's run off, no, I don't believe she would do that. Where would she go? Her family all live in this area, what she has left of them."

"Has she ever mentioned whether she is happy at home or not?"

Frowning, Nadine shook her head. "No, I presume she is. Why? Are you saying that she isn't?"

"That's what we're trying to figure out. Does she have a boyfriend?"

"No, not that she's told me."

"We're aware that she lost her aunt recently. Can you tell us how badly that affected her? Did she open up to you about how she felt?"

"Not really. I mean, we knew she was upset, and I know she changed her profile picture on Facebook to reflect how much she was missing her aunt, but I think she got over it fairly quickly. At least, I believe she did."

"What about her schoolwork, is that back on track?"

"I think so. Perhaps you'd be better off asking her dad these questions rather than me."

"May I ask why? When you're supposed to be one of her best friends?"

She ran her hand around her face and groaned. "I don't know all the answers. Why should I? Friends don't always have to tell one another every little detail in their lives."

"I know. I'm sorry. All we're trying to do is build up a picture of Sophie's life. I only have a few more questions, if that's okay?"

"All right. There's no guarantee that I'll be able to answer them, though. I'm doing my best but I'm struggling."

"That's all we can ask of you. Has Sophie mentioned if she's been in any kind of trouble lately?"

Nadine held Sara's gaze. "What type of trouble? You're going to need to give me more than that."

Sara sighed. "That's what we're trying to work out. Has she expressed any concerns?"

"No, I don't think so. Not lately. She was upset about losing her aunt, but that was weeks ago."

"Has she ever hinted about running away before? Do you think that was ever on the cards?"

"No, never. Why would she, when she lives in a beautiful home and has everything she needs?"

"To be honest, we're struggling to find another reason for her going missing."

"Someone has taken her, haven't they? There's no way she'd run off, I'm sure about that."

"And you haven't seen anyone hanging around when you've been together?"

"No, I can't remember seeing anyone, but I wasn't really looking for anyone either. I just want my friend back. I don't think you sitting around here asking questions is going to help, do you?"

"Actually, I do. This interview has given us a feel for what might have been going on in Sophie's life. I admit, speaking with you hasn't given us any leads as to where she might be, however, interviewing her friends and family might lead us along the right tracks, eventually. Is there anything else you'd like to tell us?"

Nadine's chin dipped to her chest. "No, I don't think so. I'm scared about what's going to happen to her. If she'd been kidnapped, wouldn't the kidnappers contact her father, demanding money, a ransom?"

"It's not always the case. Sometimes people, especially girls in their teens, are specifically targeted... I'll leave it there."

Nadine's head shot up, and Sara could see the sudden fear in her eyes.

"What? You think she might have been taken to work in the sex trade?"

"I didn't say that, but I have to admit, that might be a possibility, one that we'd be foolish to rule out either at this stage or further down the line. Again, I can't emphasise enough how important it is to speak with the people close to her, such as yourself."

Nadine released a shuddering breath that made the hairs on the back of Sara's neck stand to attention.

"I don't know anything, but now my mind is thinking all sorts of things. Situations that I'd rather not think about. Poor Sophie, I hope you find her soon. Are we finished now? I need to visit the toilet. I don't like crying in public."

Sara smiled and placed her hand over Nadine's. "Try not to overthink things. I'm going to leave you my card. If anything should come to mind, don't hesitate to get in touch with me."

"Thanks. I'll be sure to contact you if I hear any of the other students talking about her."

41

"One final question. Is there any bullying going on at the school?"

"Not that I know of. Sophie would never have allowed herself to have been bullied, she's got too much spirit in her. What am I saying? Where was her spirit when someone kidnapped her?"

"Maybe she showed some spirit if she was abducted, I guess we won't know the answer to that until we find her. Can you send Amy in now?"

"Okay." Nadine walked to the door and closed it behind her.

"Not sure what to make of her. What do you think?" Sara whispered.

"There was something there that wasn't sitting right with me."

"Let's see what her friend has to say. She's taking her time." Sara rose from her seat with the intention of fetching the teenager but returned to her chair when Amy entered the room. "Ah, there you are, I was coming to look for you."

"Sorry, I was comforting Nadine, she's really upset. I told her I would meet her in the loos. Will this take long?"

Sara noted that Amy's tone was clipped. "It won't, I promise. Please, take a seat."

Amy sat and then shifted her position a few times, crossing and uncrossing her legs as if she were nervous. "What do you want to know? Not that I know anything."

"Just the basics really, if you had noticed a change in Sophie's demeanour recently."

"Yeah, when her aunt died, but she was getting back to her old self again. She kind of disappeared into her shell, put the shutters up for a few weeks. Asked us to back off, to leave her alone while she dealt with her grief. We were happy to do it and pleased when she got over it."

Sara's mobile rang. She eyed the screen and groaned

42

inwardly. "Sorry, I'm going to have to take this. Sergeant, do you mind taking over?"

Carla nodded, and Sara left the room.

"Hello, DI Sara Ramsey. How may I help you, Mr Todd?"

"Oh, hi. I'm checking in with you to see how the investigation is progressing."

"So far so good, I would say. We're at the school, interviewing Sophie's two friends, Nadine and Amy."

"Good. Have they told you anything yet?"

Sara cast her eyes down the long corridor and leaned against the wall. "It's early days yet. I'm sure you're aware how difficult it is to get teenagers to open up to you."

"Ah, yes, that's right. It's the bane of my life. Sophie only tends to speak to me when she wants something. The art of conversation is lacking otherwise. What about the two men? Have you visited them yet?"

"We have. I'm sorry to report that I don't believe either of them is behind your daughter's disappearance."

"What? How do you know that?"

"We've checked out their alibis," she said, aware that he might kick off if she hadn't told him. "They were both otherwise engaged when your daughter went missing."

"We don't know the exact time of Sophie's disappearance, do we?"

"Let's put it this way then, I was satisfied with the information we gained about the two men after their confrontation with you at your office."

"What utter bullshit."

"If that's what you believe, there's little further I can say that I think will change your mind. I need to get back to work now, I have a teenager I need to urgently question. Enjoy the rest of your day."

He grunted and muttered an expletive then hung up on her.

43

Sara inhaled and exhaled a couple of deep breaths before she returned to the room.

Amy seemed to have relaxed in her absence.

"Sorry about the interruption. How are you getting on?" Sara asked Carla.

"I've been going through the usual list of questions. Amy hasn't been able to tell me much so far."

"Sorry about that. You're not going to hold it against me, are you?" Amy said. "I'm doing my best here. I can't help being nervous. I've never spoken to a police officer before."

Sara gave the girl a smile, trying to put her at ease. "We're normal people, just carrying out a job. There's no need for you to feel nervous." She reached for Carla's notebook to check Amy's answers.

"I bet you would have felt the same way I do before you became a copper. My dad always says a policeman or woman isn't to be trusted."

Sara glanced up from the notebook and inclined her head. "Is there a reason why your father would say that? Has he been in trouble with the police in the past?"

"Only minor traffic offences. He got caught doing ninety on the motorway once."

"Were you in the car at the time?"

"Yeah, me and my mum. It didn't feel like we were going that fast. Mum battered him after the police had finished with him. He got points on his licence, not sure if he got a fine as well. Mum was livid he'd been so dumb."

"And yet your father blamed the police, even though he was travelling at twenty miles over the speed limit. Can you see where I'm going with this, Amy?"

"Yeah, okay. Sorry, I'm getting better. I feel more relaxed than when I first came in."

"That'll be because I've been gentle with you," Carla stated.

"I knew I was leaving you in safe hands," Sara said. "Is there anything else we've yet to cover, Sergeant?"

"The only topic I haven't touched on is if Sophie was subjected to any form of bullying either at the school or outside."

Amy shook her head. "No, I don't think she's ever been through any of that crap. Bullies only tend to pick on weak people; no one could class Sophie as being that. She's one of the strongest girls I know. She's well liked by the other pupils in our year. There's talk of us all joining in the search for her after school plus, they're talking about holding a vigil before we set off."

"Oh, this is the first we've heard about it."

"Shit!" Amy mumbled. "Maybe it was supposed to be a secret. I'm always being told I've got a big mouth."

Sara laughed. "I like interviewing people with big mouths, it makes our lives a lot easier. When is this search going to take place?"

"It's lined up to go ahead this evening. The whole class is taking part, and they're trying to get as many of their friends in other classes to join us."

"That's amazing. What that proves to us is how well Sophie is thought of by you and the other pupils at this school."

"She is. We're all gutted she's gone missing, that's why we're doing something proactive about it. You're not going to try and stop us, are you?"

"Not in the slightest. But I will add a word of caution for everyone, to keep your wits about you. Don't let your guards down at all during the search."

"Why? Oh, hang on, I get it, you think the kidnappers might be still hanging around the school and might seize the opportunity to take someone else, is that it?"

"Possibly. We're at a loss to know what we're dealing with

yet, but I need you and your friends to remain vigilant, none-theless."

"I don't think there will be a problem, not with the nights being so light during the summer."

Sara shrugged. "I bet Sophie said the same, and yet she has gone missing."

"Damn, I never thought about that. Okay, I'll pass on your concerns to my friends when we meet up later. Is there anything else? I need to check on Nadine, see how she is."

"No, I believe we've covered everything for now. You're free to go. I'll give you one of my cards, should you think of anything else that we might need to know. Thanks for speaking with us today."

"It was tough to start with, but you both put me at ease, thank you for that. I must go. Nadine isn't good in a crisis. Sophie's usually the one who manages to calm her down. I just hope I prove to be a good substitute."

"I'm sure you're more than capable."

Amy left the room. Sara leaned back and blew out a breath.

"Anything wrong? Who called you?" Carla leaned forward to ask.

"Todd. He's going to become a thorn in my side pretty darn quickly if we fail to come up with some answers soon."

Carla sighed and shook her head. "That's so unfair. He must realise how idiotic it is to keep ringing you every few hours. You need to stamp that out, quick smart."

"Any suggestions how I'm supposed to do that are grate-fully received."

"Er... pass." Carla grinned.

"I get the sense he's going to demand to receive answers every step of the way, which is going to drive me nuts."

"I'm sorry, Sara. It's totally uncalled for. He needs to be

told that his interference is only going to hinder our progress."

"And I suppose I'm going to have to be the one to tell him, am I?"

"Or pass the buck and get Price to have a word with him."

Sara contemplated Carla's suggestion. "Hey, that's not a bad shout. Okay, I think we're finished here. I'm keen to check how the girls are, though, so might stop off at the toilets on the way out."

Carla stood and returned the chairs to their former positions. "Good idea."

They headed up the hallway and stopped when they saw Nadine and Amy come out of the toilets laughing. They spotted Sara and Carla and stopped instantly.

"Everything all right, girls?" Sara called out.

"Yes, Nadine got soaked by a faulty tap, we've been trying to mop up the mess."

"Ah, that's unfortunate. Stay safe, girls."

Nadine and Amy put their heads together and, still giggling, tore up the corridor to return to their classroom. *Hmm... there's something suspicious about their behaviour.*

Sara decided to visit the toilet before they left the school. She wasn't surprised to find the toilets clean and tidy. "Strange."

"What is? They told you they had cleaned it up," Carla replied, sticking up for the girls.

"Well, I must say, they've done an exceptional job, for teenagers."

"I'm sensing a note of sarcasm in your tone."

Sara smiled. "Since when doesn't a faulty tap spray the mirror behind the sink? See for yourself, there's not a drop left on that glass. How many teenagers do you know, who are that expert at cleaning glass?" She took a step towards the sink and touched it. She held up her dry finger. "And bone-dry, too. It's a bloody miracle. I haven't witnessed one of those in a long time."

"What are you saying? The girls lied?"

Sara cocked an eyebrow. "Let me contemplate that for an instant. Er... yes. The question is, why?"

Carla took a step forward and opened the bin. "It's empty."

Sara winked at her. "Let's get back to the station and carry out some more research on all three of their social media accounts. Something isn't adding up to me."

THE TEAM HADN'T HAD much joy either while they'd been out. Carla took over from Christine who had been searching Sophie's accounts on Facebook and Instagram, while Sara dipped into her office and rang Mark.

"Hey, can you talk?"

He laughed. "Last time I checked I could."

"Funny. You're such a scream. I'm splitting my sides here."

"All right, there's no need to go over the top. How has your day been so far?"

"Eventful, frustrating. I could go on, but that's not why I'm calling you. How are you doing?"

"I'm fine—so far anyway. I've had a relatively easy surgery this morning. A couple of garter snakes with a blockage, a kitten who needed a claw removing and a parrot who has suddenly stopped talking to its owner after fifty-three years."

"What? Do they live that long?"

"Some do, depends on how well they're cared for. I've known a couple to live until they were in their seventies. I told the owner that it was probably old age and Percy might be winding down now."

"You didn't!"

"Of course I didn't, what do you take me for?"

Sara tutted. "It's good to have the old Mark back. I've missed him over the past few months."

"About that... I'm so sorry, Sara. No matter what was going on with me physically, I had no right taking it out on you."

"Hey, you didn't. Well, maybe a little bit. It's fine, you've had an awful lot on your plate with your mum's brain tumour to contend with, as well."

"You've just reminded me, I need to give Dad a call later to see how they're both getting on. Mum wasn't feeling too good over the weekend. I told him to get an appointment at the doctor's, whether she wanted one or not. You know how stubborn she can be at times."

"She doesn't like putting people out or causing unnecessary worry."

"I'm not 'people'," he snapped, "I'm her damn son."

"Hey, there's no need to say it like that. I never meant to cause you any offence."

"I know. Right, I have to go now. My next patient is here. I'll see you later. No idea what we're going to have for dinner."

"Okay, I haven't thought that far ahead either. I love you, Mark."

"I know you do."

He upset her by hanging up without saying the three little magic words in response. But she didn't have time to dwell on that because her mobile rang, and Mr Todd's number flashed up on her screen.

Jesus, it's been less than two hours since you rang me. Give a girl a break, for God's sake.

"Hello, DI Sara Ramsey speaking. How may I help?"

"Inspector, it's Ray Todd again, and no, I've not rung up to pester you."

"Oh, then what can I do for you, Mr Todd?"

"I've arranged to hold a press conference at my surgery this evening and I think it would be good if you came along and showed your support."

"What? You can't do something like that without consulting the SIO dealing with your case, sir."

"Too late, I've done it and I'm informing you about it now."

Sara closed her eyes and bit down on the vicious retort that had sprung into her mind. "It's not the way I prefer to do things, Mr Todd."

"I'm aware of that, but it's *my* daughter who is missing, and I am going to do everything I can to try and find her. As you rightly told me earlier, time is of the essence. Will you attend or not?"

She resisted the temptation to sigh and asked, "What time?"

"Five-thirty. Can you make it?"

"I'll be there. I have to advise you against doing things like this behind my back in the future, sir, just so we're clear on that."

"Whatever. I know this was my call; I believe it's the right one. We need to strike while the iron is hot, don't you agree?"

"I would have arranged a press conference in the next couple of days if nothing had surfaced before then."

"So, what you're effectively telling me is that you believe I've jumped the gun."

"Not at all. We'll discuss it later, amongst other things."

"Such as?"

"I'll be there for five-twenty, how's that?"

"Sounds good to me. See you then."

She ended the call, picked up her pen and threw it across the room and let out a scream.

Carla entered her office a few seconds later. "Is there something wrong?"

"I'm just letting off some steam. I'm a good person, aren't I?"

Carla sat in the seat opposite. "Hey, of course you are. Has someone upset you?"

Sara raised an eyebrow. "I'll give you three guesses."

"Shit! Has Todd been on the phone again? This is getting out of hand now, you need to do something about it before it becomes a genuine problem, Sara."

"Too late, it's already reached that stage."

Carla frowned and sat forward. "Bugger, what's he done now?"

Sara growled. "Apart from blighting my life... he's only gone and called a press conference for this evening and demanded that I attend."

"What? Can he do that?"

"He's a sodding MP, someone who believes he's above the law, obviously. What an absolute arsehole."

"I totally agree. What time?"

"Five-thirty. Lucky it wasn't any later, otherwise I would have told him where to shove his invitation."

"Invitation? I thought you said he demanded you should be there."

"However you want to dress it up, it amounts to the same thing. He wants me there, by his side while he stands in front of the cameras and announces to the world that his daughter is missing."

Carla chewed her lip and raised a hand. "Now don't go biting my head off, but isn't he only doing what you'd have done yourself in the next day or so, anyway?"

Sara's eyes widened. "Wow, really? You don't think his actions are out of order?"

"Should I? Sorry if that's not what you want to hear. Maybe him putting the announcement out there himself will get more of a response than if you had to go through the ordeal."

Sara closed her eyes briefly and exhaled. "Maybe you're right. I don't know, I suppose I feel cornered, as though he's forcing my hand, pressing me to do my job."

"I don't think so. He's a father trying to do everything in his power, using the media, to reach out to the people who have taken his daughter."

"If that's what has truly happened. What if she's run off? What if there is more to this story than meets the eye? What if...? What if...? I could go on and on, the fact is, I sense things are only going to get worse with him if I don't put my foot down."

"I can appreciate both sides of the argument, if there is one. You're definitely in a tough situation, damned if you say something, like putting him in his place, and damned if you don't, because he's going to think you're a pushover and aren't up to leading the investigation. Why don't you do as I suggested earlier and run this past DCI Price?"

"Because I don't want her to think I can't handle the pressure when it comes to dealing with our local MP."

You don't know how she's likely to react unless you try. These are extenuating circumstances. My guess is that she'll be on your side, no matter what."

"Okay, you've convinced me. I'll go and see her. Do me a favour, while I'm gone, see if there is any dirt you can dig up about Todd."

Carla rolled her eyes. "How long are you going to give me? Knowing what MPs are like... no, I don't think I'll finish that sentence."

They both laughed and were still at it when they left the office much to the surprise of the rest of the team.

Sara glanced at the others and said, "You don't want to

know, I promise you. Right, I'm off to see the boss. I won't be long, I hope. In the meantime, keep digging."

"HELLO, Mary. Any chance I can have a quick word with her?" she asked DCI Price's secretary.

"Let me check her diary. She'll shoot me if I let you in every time you show up without an appointment."

"Oops, sorry. I do tend to do that a lot, don't I?"

"My lips are sealed. No, they're not. You're in luck, she's just finished the call she was on and she's not due to see or speak to anyone else for the next ten minutes. Let me see if she's made any other plans before I allow you to enter."

"That'd be great." Sara paced the area until the older woman returned.

Mary winked and pushed the office door open wider. "DCI Price has five minutes to spare, Inspector, she'll see you now."

"Thanks, Mary. A cup of your fine coffee wouldn't go amiss, if you have the time?"

"Leave it with me."

"Sara, come in and join me. What's this all about? I thought everything was going great with you up until a couple of days ago, during our last meeting. Mark hasn't had a relapse, has he?"

"Forgive the intrusion, boss. No, it's nothing like that. It's your advice I'm after, really."

"That's a first. Come in and take a seat."

Sara sat opposite her. Suddenly her nerves spiked to a level she hadn't known before. "It's like this, ma'am... I umm..."

DCI Price frowned, laid the pen she was holding on the desk and clasped her hands together. "Come on, this isn't like you, Sara, spit it out. Oh God, you're not going to tell me you're pregnant, are you? I mean, you're entitled to take time off for maternity leave, but what the hell will the team do without you and your amazing expertise?"

Sara laughed, and her nerves unravelled a touch. "Don't be so ridiculous. Mark and I have agreed that kids aren't on the agenda for us, either now or in the future."

"Good. I mean, that's a shame, but the news has come as a relief to me. So, if it's not about that, pray tell me why you're here then."

"Umm… it's to do with the new case I've taken on."

"Which is?"

"That of a missing schoolgirl."

"I'm sensing there's more to this story than just that, otherwise you wouldn't be here, would you?"

"You know me so well. There's not much that gets past you, is there?"

"You should know that by now. Out with it."

Mary chose that moment to enter the room, giving Sara the extra few seconds she needed to mull over what she wanted to say, or more to the point, how she wanted to say it and still sound professional and not like a whining bitch.

"Enjoy," Mary said and left them to it.

Sara reached for her cup.

"Leave it where it is for a moment and tell me," her boss ordered.

"The girl isn't any ordinary schoolgirl, she's Ray Todd's daughter."

"I know the name but where do I know it from?"

"He's our local MP."

"Shit, how stupid of me. I apologise, you shouldn't have had to tell me that. I'm guessing there's an issue, apart from the obvious."

"Yes, sort of. While I understand how concerned he is about his daughter, he keeps ringing me every other hour.

I'm not sure how I'm supposed to conduct my investigation with him breathing down my neck like this."

"Jesus, and what? You're here to ask me to warn him off?"

Sara cringed. "Not in so many words. I was looking for guidance on what to do about it, if anything."

"Well, you can't possibly work under those conditions, even Sherlock Holmes didn't have to put up with that shit. Have you tried speaking with him?"

"Tried and failed. The last conversation I had with him, which happened to be just before I arrived, he told me he'd arranged a press conference for this evening."

Price's head jutted forward. "He's done what? Without your prior knowledge or authority?"

"That's right. We've only been dealing with the case since first thing this morning, and he's already throwing his dummy out of the pram and going behind my back."

Price covered her face with her hands and muttered a few expletives. Her hands dropped to the desk, and she said, "He's got to be stopped. We can't have members of the public calling their own press conferences, interfering with an ongoing investigation, whether he's well known or not. It's not the done thing. More to the point, I won't allow him to ride roughshod over you. I know you said you didn't want me to intervene, but I'd be more than willing to. You shouldn't have to put up with a parent breathing down your neck six or seven times a day during an investigation, especially through the early stages, when every second matters."

"Thank you, I totally agree."

"Are you going to attend the press conference?"

"I've been instructed to. I also told him that we need to have a chat afterwards, to go over a few things. In all honesty, I think I should deal with the issue myself. I suppose what I'm saying is, I wanted you to be aware of what was going on, before things kick off."

"And you think they're likely to?"

"Don't you? He's an influential public figure. I've had brief dealings with him in the past, and to say it was distasteful would be an understatement."

"I'm sorry to hear that, Sara. Let me deal with him then, you have enough on your plate as it is."

Sara debated whether to allow Price to go into battle for her or to just have the balls to go ahead and confront Todd herself. "I think I should do it, otherwise he might see it as a weakness, me coming to you, telling tales."

"Then I think you're worrying unnecessarily. Let me rephrase that: regarding my part in this, I will continue to back you all the way. You're one officer who I always leave to get on with your work. You've rarely, if ever, let me down, Sara. Saying that, if you need me to step in and deal with him over the coming few days, don't be afraid to ask."

"Thank you for backing me, boss. It means a lot."

"Always, now drink up, and then you can tell me what's going on at home, or more to the point, how Mark is coping after his operation."

"He's fine. The doctor has allowed him to return to work, but only part-time."

Price raised an eyebrow. "I can't see him sticking to that, can you?"

"Not at all. He's advertised for a part-time vet to assist him, but there's a shortage of trained vets in the area."

"Such a shame. Okay, wish him well from me. I have another call due in a few minutes and I have to make some notes for it."

"I can drink it outside if you'd rather be left alone?"

"Yes, do that, if you don't mind."

Sara stood and made her way towards the door. "Thanks for squeezing me in, boss."

"No problem. Be firm but polite with him, Sara. Hold on

to your temper at all times. The last thing I need is any more complaints showing up on my desk. If you're having trouble dealing with him then don't be afraid to send the MP my way."

"Thanks. I'll be sure to do that."

She left the office and downed the rest of her drink within a couple of gulps, leaving the dirty cup and saucer next to the coffee machine. "You've been a life saver, as usual, Mary. See you soon."

"Not too soon, I hope, Inspector."

Sara walked the length of the corridor with the chief's reassuring words ringing in her ears. She was ready for what lay ahead of her that evening, but first, there was a whole lot of digging that needed to be done.

CHAPTER 3

*I*s that all you've found on him?" Sara asked her partner. They were coming up to the end of their shift, although Sara still had the conference to attend.

"Yep, it's not much, is it?"

Sara stared at the screen, at the minor indiscretion Ray Todd had collected during his tenure as an MP. Apparently, according to the local press, he'd been in trouble with a few of the councillors after he turned up at the local council office and threw a pot of paint around the room.

"What a tosser, all because he thought the public offices were due a renovation."

"Exactly, it doesn't make sense, does it? It's nothing to do with him."

"Not making excuses for him, but I went there a few months ago because I had a problem with my Council Tax, and I have to admit, it was looking rather shabby down there. But that doesn't mean he was in the right, forcing their hands, damaging the area with a pot of paint. Whose money will it come out of in the end? That's right, ours. He's a jumped-up little shit, isn't he? And yes, that's me being polite."

"Someone you're going to need to be wary of. I'm glad the chief has your back; I suspect things could get dicey if he doesn't get his own way."

"Christ, don't say that, I'm due to meet him in less than half an hour. How are things progressing with the three girls' social media accounts?"

"Between us, we've dug deep and have failed to find anything of importance over the past year or so. We didn't bother going back further than that, but we will, if that's what you want."

Sara sighed and shook her head. "Nope, I think it would be a waste of time. Any mention of bullying at the school in the press?"

"No, nothing at all. It's a private school; maybe they have ways of dealing with it internally."

"Possibly. How many pupils are there at the school, any idea?"

"It's relatively small in my opinion, around three hundred."

"Any other issues shown up regarding the workings of the school via the press or social media?"

"Nada. Absolutely nothing."

"Okay. Oliver, did you get a chance to go through any CCTV footage around the school?"

"I did, boss. Nothing showed up at all. I spotted Sophie leaving the school with a group of girls, but they took a shortcut through an alley, close to the school, which meant I lost them not long after."

"Where does the alley lead to?"

"A housing estate. No cameras on there for us to use to our advantage."

"That's a shame. We still have no idea when or where she

went missing. Mr Todd didn't leave work until late. So, we're looking at around a four-to-five-hour gap between her leaving school and him arriving home."

"That's a lot of hours to cover," Barry said.

Sara nodded. "It sure is. Right, I'm going to deal with any late emails that have come my way during the afternoon and then shoot off. You guys finish up here and go home, we'll start over in the morning. Hopefully, we might get an influx of calls coming in overnight that will need our attention. I hope for his sake he has arranged for someone to man the phones. He can't expect us to do it, not when he goes ahead and makes these kinds of arrangements behind my back."

"You tell him," Carla said. She punched the air with her fist.

Sara nudged her partner and left her seat to return to her office. She had ten minutes spare, but instead of going through her emails, she sat at her desk and made a few notes about the topics she intended to cover when she met up with Todd at his office.

The list grew and grew until she checked the time. "Damn, I hope the traffic isn't bad, I'm going to be late."

She shot out of her chair and flew through the outer office with her jacket, phone and handbag in hand. "Have a good evening, folks. Wish me luck."

"Good luck."

"Knock 'em dead, boss."

"You'll be fine. Drive carefully."

The team shouted after her. She was nearing the bottom of the stairs when Carla called out, "Hey, don't take any shit from him."

"I don't intend to. See you in the morning. Go home."

"I'll watch out for the news later."

"Grr... I forgot about that aspect of things. Is my hair okay?"

"You always look fine. Have fun."

"I doubt it. See you."

THE CAR PARK outside the MP's office was full, and there were no available spaces in between the double yellow lines. Sara groaned and decided to pull her trump card. She fished out the sign she generally placed on the car in dire emergencies and put it on the dashboard. 'On duty police officer'.

That should keep any traffic wardens sweet who are doing the rounds at this time of night.

"Naughty you, Inspector. Taking advantage of your position again, are you?"

Despite the smile she issued to the young reporter who had recently given her a rough time during the last press conference he'd attended, she groaned inside. "Hello, Matt, fancy meeting you here. Running late the same as me, are you?"

"Nope, I've been here for the past twenty minutes, hence me parking legally. You want to try it sometime, Inspector."

"Unlike yours, my schedule is pretty full on most days."

He sniggered at her retort and shot inside the building ahead of her. Sara followed him into what turned out to be an overcrowded room. She was amazed to see the attendance for the conference, but then she shouldn't have been, given who Todd was.

Talking of which, Todd spotted her loitering in the doorway and gestured for her to join him. Sara weaved through the crowd of journalists, who were all standing, and made her way to the front of the room.

"Nice of you to join me, even if you're a little late, Inspector," Todd whispered in her right ear.

"Sorry, I did my best to get here on time, but the traffic was bad."

"A feeble excuse at best. I would have thought a professional of your calibre would have made allowances for the traffic at this time of day. Never mind, you're here now."

"I was hoping to have a word with you in quiet before the conference began," Sara said.

"I'm afraid that opportunity has passed you by, Inspector, because unlike you, when I say a meeting goes ahead at a certain time, I make sure I stick to it."

He smiled and addressed the crowd, leaving Sara feeling like he'd delivered a sucker punch to her stomach.

"Thank you to all of you for attending this conference at short notice, I'm delighted by the turnout we've received. For those of you who aren't aware, my daughter went missing yesterday evening. I've called this conference in the hope that someone, a member of the public, will have seen her." Todd pointed at the large photo he had plastered to the wall behind him, presumably in case anyone had missed it. "I'm working closely with the police. This is Inspector Sara Ramsey, the officer in charge of the case. I know I'm in safe hands; she and her team have an excellent reputation in matters of this nature. The floor is yours, Inspector."

Todd sat, and Sara immediately stood.

"Thank you, Mr Todd. I'd like to express my concern for Sophie's welfare. After speaking with her friends and family, I have learnt that it is out of character for her to go missing like this. We're trying to remain positive at this stage but we're desperate to know what, if anything, has happened to Sophie. To our knowledge, she hasn't been involved in an accident, therefore we're reliant on what the public has to tell us. Can you help?" Sara sat, deliberately keeping her statement brief and to the point. She felt his gaze boring into the side of her face.

Finally, he said, "We're open to questions."

"Inspector, what do you believe has happened to Sophie?

Where has your investigation led you so far?" a female reporter at the front of the group asked.

Sara stood once more so the journalists at the back were able to see and hear her. "We've covered the basics up to now. Visited her school, spoken to her friends and family, and I must reiterate, as yet, I haven't uncovered any reason why Sophie should have gone missing."

"That's not what I asked, Inspector. What do you believe has happened to her?" the young female journalist insisted.

"Until further information comes our way, we're trying not to speculate what is behind her disappearance."

The questions came thick and fast, each one of them directed at Sara instead of Todd. She glanced his way and spotted what she considered to be a smirk twisting his mouth. Come the end, her head couldn't take any more, and she asked the journalists to direct any further questions at Mr Todd.

"Who called the press conference, you or the Inspector, Mr Todd?" asked Matt, the journalist who had confronted Sara outside.

"I did, with Inspector Ramsey's backing."

What the fuck? How dare you say that, knowing that I can't deny it publicly with the cameras rolling? You're insane and an arsehole. My first instinct of you was totally justified.

"Has your daughter been okay at home lately? Was there any hint of her being unhappy?" Matt asked.

Sara was beginning to like this man, especially if he was prepared to turn the screws on Todd.

"Sophie has been what I would call a normal teenager. There was a death in our family about a month ago. In my opinion she handled that situation very well, and there was no cause for concern on my part."

Matt made some notes, and with his head still down, he asked, "Any bullying going on at this private school of hers?"

"Of course not. There are no shenanigans like that going on at St Matthew's. If that were the case, I would have withdrawn my daughter from the school immediately."

"How the privileged live," someone in the crowd muttered.

Todd's expression was a picture, and Sara had to suppress the snigger threatening to emerge.

"I think we've said enough now," Todd announced. "Thank you again for attending at short notice. Please, if a member of the public has seen my daughter, will you contact the police immediately?"

Todd left his seat and exited the room. He turned in the doorway and shouted, "Inspector, if you wouldn't mind joining me for a moment before you leave."

Sara nodded and followed him as the journalists filed out of the door at the rear of the room.

Todd was pacing the floor in what appeared to be his office. Sara closed the door behind her but remained in the same position, wondering what he was so incensed about.

"Was that necessary?" he demanded.

Sara decided to play dumb. "I'm sorry? What are you talking about?"

"You clamming up like that. You should have been in charge of that conference, not me."

Sara wagged her finger. "Had I called the press together in the first place, then yes, I would have been the one doing all the talking. You took that decision out of my hands."

"The one reason I did that was to ensure my daughter is found quickly."

"And my team and I are trying to ensure the same, which is difficult to do if you insist on constantly ringing me every few hours."

"I have a right, as her father, her guardian, her sole parent, to know that my daughter's disappearance is being treated as a priority by the police. By the officer in charge of the investigation—that's you, in case you need reminding."

"I don't. My team and I have been working non-stop all day to sift through what little evidence we have that your daughter has gone missing. Let's be clear about one thing here, we're in the dark as to what time she was last seen yesterday or where. Unlike other cases my team and I have dealt with in the past. Without that valuable information to hand, it makes the investigation that much harder from the outset. Let's be fair, you haven't given me a chance to get the investigation going yet."

He continued to pace the floor. It was clear that he was getting hot under the collar, judging by the way the colour had flooded into his cheeks.

"I can see you're getting yourself worked up about this. It's not going to get us very far if you fail to remain calm."

He stopped to glare at her. "*Remain calm*, with my fifteen-year-old daughter missing? Me imagining the worst about who has taken her?"

Sara raised a hand. "With all due respect, sir, we don't know that's the case at all. Sophie might well have gone missing of her own accord."

"What utter bullshit, Inspector. Sophie would have no need to run away. She is well cared for at home, and all her needs are met adequately by me."

"I'll have to take your word for that, Mr Todd."

"I take it your staff will be working through the night to ensure any leads that come in from the conference are dealt with immediately?"

"I'm sorry, it doesn't work like that. Had I been the one to have called the conference, I would have ensured that I had obtained the necessary permission from my senior officer to use overtime for the specific purpose of manning the phones. There have been unmanageable cuts made to the Force that we have to contend with on a daily basis. Our station is under severe strain to work within the limits that have been set by the government, as I'm sure you're aware of as our local MP."

She felt his eyes bore into her very soul and could imagine the cogs churning, searching for a suitable rebuttal. It failed to appear.

Instead, he made his way to his desk and sat. "I'm sorry, I thought I was doing the right thing. That's all I ever try to do for Sophie, the right thing, for her, for us as a family."

Sara sat in the chair opposite him. "I can appreciate that. But you're going to have to allow me to conduct the investigation my way. Permit me to do my job properly without interference. The first day a person goes missing can be the most important. It's imperative that we gather the information from those close to your daughter in a swift manner."

"I know. I should have allowed you to have got on with your job, I can see that now. Have you uncovered anything at all during the day?"

"Nothing that has given us any clues as to why Sophie should have gone missing in the first place. Are you aware that a vigil was being held at the school this evening?"

He stared at her and shook his head. "No, I wasn't." His head dipped.

"After which, the pupils were going to carry out a search of their own for Sophie."

"They're doing that? Going out of their way to look for my daughter?"

"They are. From the information we've been able to gather so far, Sophie appears to be a bright and well-liked pupil at her school. The staff and the rest of her classmates wanted to show how much she means to them."

"And here I am, organising a press conference behind

your back, expecting you to attend and be okay with it. I've screwed up, haven't I?"

Sara shrugged. "What's done is done. What you're going to have to do going forward is trust me. Discuss things with me before you go ahead and organise anything yourself."

"I realise I was in the wrong, however," he added, his fighting spirit coming to the fore once more, "I do believe you should have called a press conference yourself."

"As I've already told you, during what we call the 'Golden Hour', although it can span over twenty-four hours or more, our time is mostly spent gathering evidence and speaking to those people who are considered close to the missing person. I believe we've successfully covered all of that today, plus we also spoke to two members of the public, Mr Wade and Mr Potts, whose names you gave me yourself and who you felt might have something to do with your daughter's disappearance. So, as you can see, my team and I haven't had a moment to ourselves today, and we definitely haven't been sitting around doing nothing."

"What about the conference and the leads you might gather from that being aired this evening?"

"We'll deal with anything we deem worthy of chasing up, first thing in the morning."

"What? You've all clocked off for the evening?"

"My team have but there will still be patrols out there looking for Sophie. They've already conducted house-to-house enquiries in the area but, unfortunately, they haven't resulted in anything."

His eyes narrowed into tiny slits, and he heaved out a breath. "Un-fucking-believable. What's the point in calling a press conference if you aren't going to take it seriously?" he shouted, ignoring her reassuring words.

She let out a long sigh. "I didn't call one. Had I been given the opportunity of doing it, I would have made the necessary arrangements for the calls to have been answered by a member of my team as I've already stated, along with gaining the permission to use the necessary overtime."

His eyes closed, and Sara sensed he was performing some form of relaxation exercise.

She left him to it for a few moments and then rose from her seat. "If there's nothing else, I need to get home."

His eyes flew open. "No, you can't do that. You need to go back to the station, be there to answer the calls."

"I don't. I need to go home to care for my husband who has recently had cancer surgery. So, if you don't mind, I'll speak to you soon."

His mouth gaped open. "Shit! I apologise. I had no idea what you were going through."

"Why would you? And I haven't, my husband is the one who has been laid up for weeks after his operation."

Stick that where the sun don't shine, mate.

Sara left the room and made her way out to her car. The time was getting on for six-thirty; she couldn't believe she had been here an hour already. Where had the time gone? Making her way towards her car, she toyed with the idea of dropping over to the school to lend her support to Sophie's friends and classmates, but the pull to spend the evening with Mark, after his first day back at work, proved to be too much for her in the end. Sara started the car and drew away. She caught a glimpse in her rearview mirror of Todd locking up his office, and was still undecided what to make of him. One minute she hated him, the next she couldn't help but feel sorry for him.

SARA KNEW she'd made the right decision to come straight home when she found Mark at the kitchen table, his head resting on his arm, fast asleep.

She gently woke him. "Mark, are you all right?"

He sat upright, his back rigid and his eyes wide open. "What's going on? Is there a fire? Where is it?"

Sara laughed. "No, there's no fire. You fell asleep in the chair. Are you okay?"

He stretched his arms above his head, yawned noisily, and then pulled her onto his lap. "I'm fine, just catching forty winks before I tackle the evening meal."

They shared a kiss.

"Why don't we go out for something to eat or grab a takeaway tonight, instead?"

"No, we've had too many takeaways over the last few weeks. They're not good for you. I can knock up one of my special omelettes if you fancy cutting up some potatoes for chips."

"Why not? Sounds like the ideal meal for me. How did work go today?"

"Same as usual. It was quieter this afternoon, giving me a chance to give Mum and Dad a call."

Sara paused after she'd removed the potatoes from the veg rack. "And, how were they?"

"Mum's not well at all. She spent most of the day in bed with a severe headache."

"Oh no, that doesn't sound too good. What did the doctor say?"

"He called round to see her, gave her a painkilling injection and told her she needed to rest. Dad told me he'd been fighting with her all day. She was determined to get out of bed, and Dad ended up sitting in the chair beside the bed, reading a book, making sure she stayed put. Eventually, Mum dropped off to sleep, and Dad was able to get out and do a bit of tidying up in the garden for half an hour or so."

"At least he managed to catch a break for himself. You know as well as I do how stubborn your mother can be."

69

"And some. Anyway, did your day improve since we spoke at lunchtime?"

"Not in the slightest. If anything, it got worse."

"What? How?"

"I'll tell you over dinner. Let's concentrate all our efforts on getting our meal ready for now, I'm starving."

"Whatever you want, you know I'm not one for pushing you."

She leaned over and kissed him. "That's why I love you so much."

"Ditto. I've got some bacon and chorizo that needs using up. Shall I chuck them in as well?"

"Why not? I love a bit of spice in my life."

"Ooer Mrs."

They both laughed.

CHAPTER 4

*S*ara drove into work with a good feeling running through her. Hopefully it meant that she was in for a better day ahead of her.

"Morning, Jeff. It's a welcome surprise not to have our MP friend waiting on the doorstep to see me first thing."

Jeff grinned. "You've just missed him."

"What? He's been here this morning?"

"Not in person, but he rang to speak with me."

"Oh God, I'm not going to like this, am I?"

"Actually, he was fine. Asked me what kind of response we'd received from the conference."

"Oh, okay, and what did you tell him?"

"That I would pass the information on to you and let you give him the good news."

Sara cringed. "And is there any good news for me to pass on?"

"Nope, nothing. The phones have been deathly silent all night."

"Shit! That's not what I was hoping to hear, but in a way, it backs up my theory about holding a conference too early."

"I agree. He was in the wrong."

"Gosh, I hope you didn't tell him that, Jeff?"

"I didn't. That's not to say I wasn't tempted to bring him down a peg or two. Who does he think he is, arranging a press conference behind your back like that?"

"Don't worry. I didn't let him get away with it. I put him in his place after the conference had finished."

"Brilliant. Just because he's our local MP, it doesn't give him the right to treat you like you're some kind of junior copper around here. That's my tuppence worth anyway, please or offend. His type makes me sick. It reeks of misogyny."

"Really? That thought never even crossed my mind. Anyway, I've had a word with DCI Price, just in case the situation gets out of hand. She'll deal with him if he oversteps the mark again, although, I genuinely believe he won't. I told him in no uncertain terms last night that I thought he'd gone too far."

"Good for you. I had a feeling you would stick up for yourself. Not that this sort of thing should be dumped on your doorstep to begin with. What does he think you do all day? Sit at your desk playing Solitaire on that computer of yours, like he probably does?"

The outer door opened, and Carla joined them. "What are you two laughing about?"

"I'll tell you on the way up. See you later, Jeff."

Carla did the honours of putting in her code to open the security door. Sara filled her in about what had happened the previous evening with Todd.

"What the fuck? He expected you to have one of us work through the night at the drop of a hat? What planet is he from?"

"I know. Don't worry, I put him straight. Hey, forget about it, I have."

"You're a better person than I am, Sara Ramsey."

"Hardly. Anyway, his underhand strategy backfired." Sara made her way over to the drinks station.

Carla switched on a few of the computers on their colleagues' desks. "What do you mean?"

"Jeff was just telling me about the lack of calls the station had received overnight, regarding Sophie Todd's whereabouts before she went missing."

"Heck. Where does that leave us then?"

"Do you want one or are you sticking with your water?"

Carla raised a finger to her lips and peered over her shoulder at the main door. "I'd love one. I don't think water and I are destined to have a lasting relationship, but don't tell Des that I've ditched my new health regime so soon."

Sara giggled. "Your secret is safe with me. As to your question, in all honesty, I'm at a loss what to do next." She prepared the drinks and delivered Carla's to her then perched on the desk near her partner. "I'm open to suggestions as to how we should proceed."

"Blimey, don't go looking at me to come up with a plan. That's far beyond my pay grade as a sergeant."

"Bugger off. You're supposed to support me, not step aside and allow me to sink."

"You're hardly doing that. We mustn't give up hope yet. Experience should tell you that we've never garnered much information in the hours immediately after a conference before, have we?"

"I suppose you're right."

The rest of the team began to arrive.

"Morning, boss. That was some press conference last night," Barry said with a smirk.

"Less said about that the better," Sara replied. She took her cup and headed towards her office. "You know where to find me if anything should rear its head."

"We do," Carla replied. "Do you want us to keep digging? Also, we've heard back from the patrols. None of the residents saw Sophie after she went down the alley, but a few mentioned the kids doing a search."

"That's disappointing. Okay, carry on digging, give me a shout when you reach the Southern Hemisphere, I could do with a few relaxing days in the sun." She chuckled and crossed the room to sit behind her desk. There was the odd brown envelope or two to deal with and around five emails vying for her immediate attention. She'd not long started replying to her emails when the phone rang. It was Jeff. "What can I do for you, Sergeant?"

"I've got a lady in reception who's a tad upset, ma'am. I wondered if you wouldn't mind coming down to speak with her."

"Is it relevant to the Sophie Todd case?"

"It might be."

"I'll be right down." She completed signing off the email she was dealing with and sent it, then left her desk. "Carla, can you bring your notebook and come with me?"

Carla glanced up from the notes she was making. "If you insist."

Outside the room, on the way back down to the reception area, Carla asked, "What's going on?"

"Jeff's asked me to speak with a woman. He's hinted that she might have some information about Sophie Todd."

"Hinted?"

"You know as much as I do."

Sara opened the door to find a woman crying. She was in her forties and sitting in the chair close to the front door.

Jeff raised an eyebrow at Sara. "This is Mrs Moses, Inspector Ramsey."

Sara and Carla both approached the upset woman.

"Hello, Mrs Moses. I'm DI Sara Ramsey, and this is my partner, DS Carla Jameson. What can we do to help?"

"I'm Isla. You can help me to find my son. He's gone missing."

"I see." Sara glanced at Jeff and asked, "Is there a room available for us to use?"

"The room behind you is free. Can I get you all a drink?"

"Mrs Moses, Isla? Would you like a tea or coffee?"

"A cup of sweet tea for me, three sugars." She sniffled and wiped her nose on a tissue she produced from her sleeve.

"Carla and I are okay, a tea with three sugars for Mrs Moses. Thanks, Jeff."

Sara opened the door immediately behind her and invited Isla to join her. She rearranged the chairs in the smallish room. "Please take a seat."

"Thank you. I don't want to be a nuisance, but I didn't know who else to turn to."

"You're not being a nuisance. Can you tell us when you saw your son last?"

"At breakfast yesterday. I had to leave early and didn't arrive home until after ten last night. Daniel is used to me working extra hours. He's capable of looking after himself. When I got home, I presumed he was tucked up in bed, but when he didn't appear for breakfast this morning, I went to check on him. His bed was empty and hadn't been slept in. Well, it didn't look as though it had."

"Does Daniel have a phone?"

"Yes. I tried to call him, but the phone went straight to voicemail. I left a message, but he hasn't got back to me, and now I'm out of my mind with worry."

"Sorry to hear that. What school does he go to?"

"St Matthew's out at Holme Lacy."

Sara winced.

"What's wrong? Do you know something I don't know?" Isla asked, panic-stricken.

"Did you see the news last night?"

"No, I went straight to bed, I was too shattered to watch TV when I got home. I'd already eaten at the office, at around seven. Why do you ask?"

"Because a couple of days ago, on Monday, a girl from Daniel's school was also reported missing."

Isla gasped and covered her face with her hands. "Oh God, what does this mean?"

Sara puffed out her cheeks. "I'm not sure. We put an appeal out to the general public last night but, unfortunately, we haven't received any response to it."

"Again, I'm asking you what you mean by that. Has someone taken our kids on purpose?"

Sara shrugged. "We can't rule anything out at this stage."

Isla began to sob. "I can't believe this is happening. Daniel is such a good boy. We've been through hell and back in the past few years, since his father left us. Oh no, this will mean I'll have to call him. He'll come back and demand to take over, even though he walked out on us because he couldn't stand being a father and 'family life wasn't for him', and yes, I'm quoting what he said when he left."

"Were they close? Daniel and his father?"

"They haven't had any contact with each other for the past couple of years, so I wouldn't call them close. Daniel has a tendency to fling his father deserting us at me, now and again, when we fall out."

"And how often does that happen?" Sara asked.

"Not that much, not in comparison to what I gleaned from my colleagues at the office. They live lives from hell most of them, compared to what I have to contend with. Daniel is very bright; he works well at school. I can't say that I've had any mischievous behaviour to deal with, especially not recently, now that he's preparing for his exams. I'm sorry, I'm waffling on here and not allowing you to get a word in edgewise."

"It's okay, we're used to it. It'll be the shock talking. I know it's not easy, but try and calm down. The more information you can give us about Daniel from the outset, the more chance we will have of finding him. Do you know if anything was worrying him?"

"No, I don't believe so. Although, he has been a bit tetchy lately. You know the type of thing, grunting an answer instead of opening his mouth and saying yes or no when I've asked him an important question."

"I'd say that was typical teenage behaviour, wouldn't you? I remember doing the same to my dad when it was coming up to exam time."

"I suppose I was the same, back in the day. I've never really thought about it that way. I'm not saying he's a bad boy, far from it. He's kind and considerate, not the type of boy who needs to be reminded when it's my birthday. He's very close to my mother, so she deals with that side of things."

"Have you tried calling any family members in the area to see if he's shown up there?"

"It's the first thing I did. Now I've got my mother all worked up about her precious grandson and threatening to stay with me until he's been found. She's the one who told me to come down here, sit in the reception area and not leave until someone was prepared to take me seriously."

"Not that you needed prompting to do that, I'm sure."

"True. You know how some parents feel it's their duty to tell you how to suck eggs, despite you being an adult for more years than you care to mention."

Sara smiled. "I do. Do you have any other relatives living in the area?"

"My brother who is older than me, but I don't really have much to do with him. He made it clear what he thought of me when I kicked Clive out. He blamed me for my marriage failing."

"I take it they used to be good friends?"

"Yes, they used to go to the local rugby matches together and watch all the sport under the sun on the blasted TV in the living room. It used to drive me potty until I insisted on us putting another TV in the snug-cum-office that I use when I'm working from home. It's warm, being quite a small room, and I can shut myself away in there, either watch the TV or read a book. Mind you, I haven't needed to do that since Daniel's father left us. Daniel has a portable TV in his bedroom that his grandparents bought him a few years ago. He tends to stay in his room most of the time these days."

"From that, I'm getting the impression you've possibly drifted apart lately. Have you?"

Isla took a sip from her drink, giving Sara and Carla the chance to do the same. "Gosh, I haven't really thought about it. God, now that I've had a chance to dissect our lives like this... I feel terrible."

"Why should you feel bad?"

"Because I've been turning more and more to work for the answers, since my failed marriage, and that's led to me neglecting Daniel..." She broke down again. "And now he's gone missing, and I can't help blaming myself." Isla plucked a tissue from the box on the table and blew her nose, then whispered, "I'm such a shit mother."

Sara shook her head. "Don't be ridiculous, you're far from it. You've done the right thing, coming here today to advise us that your son is missing."

Carla nudged Sara's knee under the table.

Sara turned and said, "Is there something you'd like to either add or ask, Sergeant?"

"Just a quick question, if I may?"

Sara nodded.

"Did your son attend the vigil for Sophie Todd after school yesterday?" Carla asked.

"Good shout," Sara encouraged.

"Umm... I didn't know there was going to be one. Has something happened to her? She's a girl in his class. I seem to remember him talking fondly about her. Wait, isn't she the local MP's daughter? Is she the one you mentioned earlier?"

"That's right. She went missing a couple of days ago, after she left school for the day. The children were holding a vigil for her at the school then setting off to try and look for her, retrace her steps after she left school."

"Oh hell, sorry if you consider me a bit slow on the uptake, my head is swirling with dozens of nightmare scenarios of what might have happened to Daniel." Her head dipped. "He didn't tell me that was his intention, to join in the search. Why wouldn't he have done that?"

"I don't know. I believe it was something the pupils them-selves came up with."

"Knowing Daniel, he'd be the first to sign up, anything to help out. He's a very sensitive lad. Always tries to do the right thing by people, young and old. He cares for his grandpar-ents a great deal, to the point that he's always the one to suggest we should go round there and see them more. My work tends to get in the way a lot of the time. When I'm not in the office, I can usually be found at home. Sometimes I don't even make it to my snug and sit at the kitchen table, paperwork spread out all around me. It drives him to despair at times."

"What do you do?" Sara asked.

"I'm the head accountant at my firm. I don't own it, but the owner is very reliant on me and, I have to say, I love my work. If I'm close to finalising reports, I refuse to leave it at the office and most of the time I complete the task at home. Why did I choose to stay behind last night and not take my work home with me?" She sighed, and fresh tears dripped onto her cheeks.

"There's no point punishing yourself. What we need to do now is find Daniel and we're going to need your help to begin the process."

"My help? Yes, of course, I'll do anything to assist you, you only have to ask."

"What about your job?"

"I rang them this morning. Told them I came down with a bug last night before I left the office. They've agreed to give me a couple of days off. I didn't want to tell them the truth because I feel ashamed that I've let Daniel down."

"Let's get one thing straight, you haven't let your son down. You're here now, reporting him missing, aren't you?"

"I am, but hours after he went missing. If only I had bothered checking on him when I got home last night. That regret will haunt me until my dying day if it turns out that something bad has happened to him."

"Okay, I need to tell you, no matter how hard this gets, you are going to need to remain positive at all times."

"I know but..."

Sara wagged her finger. "No buts. Negativity is never the answer in situations like this. I've learnt that a lot over the years."

"I'm prepared to listen to your expert advice, Inspector. Where do we go from here?"

"What we're going to need from you is a list of Daniel's friends, their contact numbers and those of his immediate family, living in the area."

"Oh God, now you're asking. I need to go back home; I have a book sitting next to the house phone that has all the relevant phone numbers in it. I'm so glad I got Daniel to put his friends' in that. We never know what's around the corner, do we? Or what we'll do if our mobiles ever pack in."

"So true. If you can get that back to us, or let us know the details ASAP, we can get the ball rolling."

"Is that it? Aren't you going to reprimand me for being the worst mother on this planet? Tear me off a strip or two for not putting my son's needs before my own?"

Sara smiled and shook her head. "Why would I? These things happen, it's how we deal with them that makes the difference, not dwelling on the numerous ifs and maybes."

"Thank you, you've at least put my mind at ease. I thought I'd be in trouble for leaving a minor at home on his own."

"Had your son been ten years younger, yes, maybe that would have been the case. Please, stop being so hard on yourself. What I will ask you is a few more basic questions, like if your son has been worried about anyone following him lately."

"He's never mentioned anything, it would have been the first thing I would have told you. To my knowledge he's never fallen out with another classmate. He goes to a private school, that type of thing doesn't go on there, at least I hope it doesn't. I'd soon remove him if I got wind of any form of trouble like that, I can tell you. Is that what you believe? That someone has kidnapped my son and this other girl, Sophie?"

"All I can tell you is that there is a possibility that might be the case, unless you're prepared to tell me that Daniel might have left home on his own accord? Did you check his room for any possible sign that he packed a bag and left?"

Isla groaned. "I'm sorry, but the thought never even crossed my mind. I didn't check if his bag was still there or not. I'm trying to recall if I saw his laptop still in the room... sorry, I can't say I noticed it. I can give you a call when I get back home and check."

"Thanks, that would be a great help. Will you call his father or would you rather I did that?"

Isla paused, and Sara could tell she was contemplating her options.

"I think it would be less damaging if the news came from me, er, if you get what I mean. He's got a bit of a temper; I'm used to being in the firing line. I know how to calm him down, or I used to be able to, at one time, at the start of our relationship. Bugger, now you've got me doubting myself. Maybe it would be better if you contacted him." She sighed. "Saying that out loud has put doubts in my mind again. What would you do if you were in my shoes?"

"Honestly, I think I would take the plunge and contact him myself. I'll give you a card, you can tell him to call me if he needs any further information. Not that we know anything else, other than what you've already told us."

Isla ran a hand around her face. The colour draining from her features was replaced by utter dread.

Sara handed Isla one of her business cards. "You've got this, but if you can't do it then please, say so now. I think the longer you leave it before telling him, the worse it is going to be for you in the long run."

"You're right. He's not going to be happy, but then I can't worry about what he thinks, my priority remains with my son. Where can he be? He's never shown any signs of being that unhappy that he would feel the need to run off."

"How close was he to Sophie, do you know?"

"I haven't got a clue. I can't say I remember him ever mentioning her name during a conversation, that's not to say he hasn't."

"Okay, you've given us enough to be going on with. We'll start digging for clues until you can supply us with the extra information about his friends and family members. We'll also need a recent photo of Daniel."

She slid back her chair and stood. "Thank you for being so kind to me and for not judging me at all. I'll cobble together what you need and get back to you soon. It's going to take me around twenty minutes to get back home again."

"We're not here to judge you, only to assist you, please remember that. The more honesty we get from a parent in cases such as this, the quicker the outcome is. And please, remember to check his bedroom, see if anything obvious is missing."

"I will, that's the first thing I'll do. Thank you again."

Sara smiled and opened the door. Isla shot through it and out the main entrance before either Sara or Carla had left the room.

"Not another one," Sara said.

"Shall I organise the team? Get them doing the usual, or how would you rather deal with this one?"

"Yes, get that sorted, then you and I need to get on the road. I want to see what Mrs Cooke has to say about this, face to face."

CHAPTER 5

*S*ara's nerves jangled the closer she got to the school. While Carla had sorted out jobs for the individual team members to carry out in their absence, Sara had rung ahead and requested an urgent meeting with the head-mistress. She agreed to see them if they showed up within the next hour. Holme Lacy was almost thirty minutes from the station, and Sara felt time was against them when they got snarled up at the traffic lights, close to the large Asda. "I'm tempted to use the bloody siren. These lights always take an eternity to change."

"Don't they just? You'd be well within your rights, if we're against the clock."

With that, the lights changed to green, and their journey got underway again. But with every set of traffic lights they encountered after that, Sara's patience got the better of her, and she grasped the steering wheel tighter. "It's true what they say, hit one on red and you're screwed for the rest of your trip."

Carla chuckled. "You're not wrong. This is getting beyond a joke. You're going to have to do it."

Sara inched her car back then forwards to get out of the gap between the car sitting in front of her and the one directly behind her and then switched on her siren and put her foot down. A couple of drivers coming in the opposite direction blasted their horn at her, but she ignored their ignorance and upped her speed. They arrived at the school with ten minutes of their allotted time to spare.

"Up for a bit of a trot?" Sara asked. She glanced down at the low heels on her ankle boots and then at Carla's flat ones. "You win. If you get there before me, apologise for us being late."

"I won't. We're in this together." Carla pointed at the exterior of the building in several locations. "There are cameras all around this place, which should be helpful."

"You'd think so, wouldn't you? We'll see if that's the case or not."

Mrs Cooke's secretary smiled when they rushed into the office.

"Sorry we're late, we got held up at every traffic light between here and the station."

"No problem. Mrs Cooke still has eight minutes before her conference call is due to happen. Let me show you in. Can I get you a drink?"

"No, thanks all the same. We had one before we left the station."

Mrs Cooke glanced up from the paperwork she was dealing with and greeted them with a cautious smile. "Come in. It's nice to see you both again. Do you have any news about Sophie?"

"Sadly, that isn't the case. I take it you haven't heard the news about Daniel Moses then?"

Mrs Cooke's brow furrowed. "Daniel, no. I've heard nothing. Although today has been rather hectic so far. Please tell me what you know?"

85

"We're assuming Daniel attended the vigil and the subsequent search that was arranged for Sophie last night?"

"I believe so. I seem to recall overhearing one of the teachers saying this morning that it was a better turnout than anyone was expecting, and all the pupils showed up in force."

"That's great to hear. Umm… with regard to Daniel, his mother turned up at the station first thing this morning to report him missing."

"She did? Let me contact his form teacher, ask her if he's in school today."

"Thank you, that would be helpful."

Mrs Cooke rang a number. "Jackie, was Daniel Moses at registration this morning…? I see, thank you. If any other students fail to show up the rest of the week, I'm to be informed immediately." She hung up and chewed her lip. "He was marked absent, and his form teacher said she asked the other pupils if they'd seen him, but they all said they hadn't. What does this mean? That two students are now on the missing list?"

"As far as we know. Mrs Moses returned home from work late last night. She assumed Daniel was fast asleep as the house was quiet so decided not to disturb him. When she shouted him down for breakfast this morning he didn't appear, and his bed hadn't been slept in. What we'd like to know is, if anything out of the ordinary happened at the event that was organised."

"I'd have to check. Mr Lawton was with the children, I believe, ensuring everything remained peaceful. I think a couple of the other teachers gave up their time to be there as well. This is the worst news imaginable. I'll need to give Mrs Moses a call, tell her she has my full support."

"I'm sure she'd appreciate that. If you could ask Mr Lawton first, before we run out of time?"

She dialled another number, and Mr Lawton joined them a few moments later.

"Ah, Mitch, can you have a word with DI Ramsey about last night? I'm sorry, time is against us, and I need to attend this conference call with the governors, otherwise my name will be mud."

"Don't worry, I'll take care of the detectives. Shall we continue this conversation in the staffroom instead?"

Sara and Carla followed him the few feet down the hallway to the empty staffroom.

"I had a free lesson, so thought I'd spend the time marking some test papers. Excuse the mess, won't you? I do tend to take up a lot of room during this task. My wife is always telling me off for messing up the house when I take this lot home with me."

Sara smiled. "Looks like my desk in the morning. Don't worry about it. Perhaps you can tell us what went on last night?"

He crossed his arms and tapped his foot. "I don't think anything out of the ordinary occurred. We held a brief vigil by the school gates and then set off to carry out a search for Sophie, in case she'd fallen over, knocked herself out in the woodland near the school. Something along those lines. A small group of friends took it upon themselves to check the woods. May I ask what all this is about?"

"Daniel Moses failed to go home last night. His mother reported him missing this morning."

"Good heavens. I wasn't expecting you to say that, not for a single moment. I hadn't heard that he'd gone missing. I spoke to a few of the pupils this morning, and no one mentioned that anything bad had happened last night. I'm assuming they would, if Daniel hadn't completed the search with them."

"That is strange," Sara agreed. "Maybe they were with him

until the end of the search, and he disappeared on the way home. Is it possible to speak to the pupils who were with him during the search?"

"Yes, do you want me to get them for you now?"

"I think that would be for the best."

He rushed out of the room.

Sara paced the floor as she thought.

"What's going through that head of yours?" Carla asked with one eye on the door.

"To be honest with you, there's so much, it's hard to choose anything that might point us in the right direction or be useful for the investigation."

Carla rubbed her eyes and then frowned. "What? Do you want to run that past me again?"

The door opened, and Mr Lawton returned with two boys. One of them was a few inches taller than his teacher.

"These are Matthew and Kevin Davis. They're Daniel's closest friends and were with him until he reached the end of his road last night."

"Hello, thanks for agreeing to speak with us. Can you tell us at what time you left him?"

The taller lad, Matthew, didn't have to consider the question for too long; he answered straight away. "It was just after seven."

"Did Daniel tell you what his plans were for the rest of the evening?" Sara asked.

"He was going to do his geography and history homework and get an early night."

"Have you heard from him since he got home?"

"No. We were expecting to see him at school this morning. He must be sick or something. It's not like him to miss school."

"Has Mr Lawton told you why we're here?"

The boys looked perplexed and shook their heads.

"No," Matthew said. "Is he all right?"

"We're not sure. His mother reported him missing this morning. Did anything unusual or out of the ordinary happen last night, while you were together?"

"No, nothing. All we were doing was concentrating on trying to find out what happened to Sophie... now he's gone missing as well." His eyes teared up.

"Sorry if this has come as a shock to both of you. Would you like to take a seat?"

"No, I'm all right," Matthew replied.

Kevin shook his head. "No thanks. What are you doing about it?"

"First, we must find out as many facts as we can gather from his family and friends, then we can begin the investigation in earnest. Are Daniel and Sophie close?"

Matthew nodded. "Kind of. She's in the same class as us, and sometimes we hang around with her and her mates."

Sara was at a loss what to ask next, so she thought she'd ask the most obvious question she could come up with. "Have either Sophie or Daniel spoken about running away together?"

The boys glanced at each other and then immediately shook their heads.

Matthew replied, "No, I don't think so."

"I don't either," Kevin agreed.

"Mr Lawton, have you ever overheard any conversations of that nature between Sophie and Daniel?"

"I can't say I have, sorry. Is that what you believe this is all about?"

"Frankly, I'm not quite sure. We're following up on both options, whether the kids have run off together, which seems unlikely, given the incidences happened a couple of days apart, or someone is abducting children from this school."

"Do you have any further questions for Matthew and Kevin, Inspector?"

"No, they can go back to their lessons now. Thank you for speaking with us, boys."

"I hope you find them," Kevin mumbled before they both left the room.

"I wish you hadn't said that in front of them," Mr Lawton said as soon as the door closed behind the boys.

"Said what?" Sara asked, confused.

"That it's possible kids are being abducted from this school."

"Ah, I see. Sorry, but it happens to be the truth. I'm not one for dancing around important issues, unlike some people. I think when we leave, you and the head should discuss having an open conversation with the kids to make them aware of the situation and encourage them to come forward if they know anything about what's going on and also to tell them to remain vigilant."

"We'll do that, don't worry. Is there anything else I can help you with?"

"Yes, in fact there is. Any chance we can view the footage from the school cameras, particularly around the time the kids set off last night?"

"I don't see why not. I'll need to pass you over to Les, he's in charge of the security around here, amongst other things. I'll take you to his room, see if he's available to have a chat with you."

"Thanks."

They followed Lawton down two corridors, and he knocked on a door halfway down the third one.

A man in his fifties opened it.

"Hi, Les. These two ladies are from the police. They're investigating the disappearances of two of our pupils and have asked to view the footage from when the search party set off last night. Can you help them out?"

"Oh, yes, of course. Come in."

"I'll be off then. Anything else you need before you go, you know where to find me."

Sara smiled. "Thanks, you've been a huge help."

"Hardly. Good luck with your investigation. I hope you find Sophie and Daniel soon."

"We hope that's the case, too."

Lawton walked away, and Les invited them into his larger-than-average security room.

"What's your role here, Les?" Sara asked.

"You name it, I tend to cover it. I suppose my real job title would be school handyman, but they also trust me to deal with the security. Now, let's find the footage you're after, shall we?"

"That'd be great. Were you here last night?"

"No, I offered to hang around, but Mrs Cooke assured me that wasn't necessary. It was my wife's birthday, and I'd arranged a surprise family dinner at a restaurant."

"That was nice of you."

"She means everything to me. We've raised four great kids together. Enough about me and my boring family." He messed around with the keyboard for a few seconds before images began to appear on the screen. "This was the vigil they held by the gates."

"Mrs Cooke wasn't kidding when she said all the kids wanted to get involved."

"I know. I was shocked when I saw how many turned up as I was leaving."

"It looks like the whole school were determined to show their respects."

"Give or take the odd one, you're right. Sophie was well liked by the other pupils. I was shocked to learn that she'd

91

gone missing and now Daniel has gone as well, it's hard to believe. Did you want to view anything else?"

"Can we view the children setting off on the search? Do you know Daniel Moses?"

"I'm probably familiar with his appearance, although I'm not really good with names."

"It doesn't matter. If you can run the footage, we'll see if we can spot him on the screen."

Sara and Carla took a step closer.

"Isn't that him?" Carla said. She pointed to a small group of boys at the back.

"Possibly, it's too hard to tell." Sara withdrew her phone and compared the image on the screen with the photo his mother had sent her earlier that morning. "Yes, that looks like him."

"Do you know when he went missing?" Les asked.

"He never made it home last night. He was last seen at around seven-thirty."

"What? Crikey, never in my days did I ever dream of hearing about two kids going missing from this school. It beggars belief. What's going on?"

"That's what we're trying to find out. Can you give us a copy of the footage so we can study it more closely back at the station?"

"I can, give me a second to sort that out for you."

Sara noted his hands were shaking. "Are you okay?"

"Not really. This news has knocked me for six."

"Sorry, I didn't mean to upset you. I take it you've never come across anything like this going on at the school before?"

"No, never. All the kids are from well-off families, though, I suppose if any kids are going to get kidnapped, the vile people taking them would come to this school rather than a state school, wouldn't they?"

Sara shrugged. "I can see your logic. The trouble is, until we figure out what the kidnappers' motive is if they've even been kidnapped, we're constantly scrabbling around for answers."

"I can only imagine how awful this must be for you to investigate. I hope in some small way I can make things easier for you by giving you the footage."

"In our experience, every little helps." Sara's mobile rang. She removed her phone from her pocket and angled it so Carla could see who was calling her. "I'll be right back. Sorry about this, it's important."

"Don't mind us, we'll plod on in here," Les said jovially.

Sara left the room and answered the call on the fourth ring. "Hello, Mr Todd. What can I do for you?"

"Why the delay in answering, Inspector? Where are you?"

Sara pulled the phone away from her ear and stared at it. *What the fuck? Who the hell do you think you are?* Putting it to her ear again, she replied, "For your information, Mr Todd, I was interviewing someone. I'm in the middle of an investigation. That means I don't sit at my desk all day, shuffling paper, like some people."

"Meaning?"

"Meaning nothing. I'm trying to tell you that I have a job to do. We discussed this last night; you're going to have to allow me to get on with my job and stop ringing me every couple of hours. I was told by the desk sergeant, when I arrived at the station this morning, that you had not long called the station to see what the response was like to the conference you had arranged."

"I did and now I'm asking you, as you weren't on duty at the time."

"Is that a dig? I'm entitled to time off, sir. Just because it's your daughter who has been reported missing, it doesn't mean that my team and I are expected to work day and night to find her when there are uniforms on hand to continue while we're off the clock. Your case is being treated the same way as any other that lands on my desk."

There was silence on the other end, apart from the odd bout of heavy breathing. "I'm sorry. All I want is my daughter to be returned home to me."

"Again, that's my objective, too, in case you hadn't noticed."

"Where are you? May I ask who you're interviewing?"

"If you must know, things have changed." She winced. Why did she tell him that?

"In what way?"

"We're back at the school, viewing the footage from the vigil they held for your daughter last night."

"Why?"

"Because when the pupils set off to search for Sophie, another boy in her class, Daniel Moses, went missing. So, we're now dealing with two missing teenagers instead of just one."

"What the...? You have to find out what's going on, Inspector. You have to."

"Believe me, I'm trying. That's why you need to back off and allow me to carry out my work properly."

"Okay, I'm sorry. I was in the wrong. Will you call me this evening, before you finish your shift?"

"For what reason?"

"To let me know how the investigation is progressing, of course."

"As I've told you, on more than one occasion, Mr Todd, an investigation doesn't work like that. You'll be informed as soon as anything major develops in your daughter's case. Until then, please give me the space I need to conduct this investigation the way I always do, to the best of my ability."

"I will. Again, I apologise for the intrusion, but you must understand things from my point of view."

"Believe me, I do. Take care, sir." She ended the call before he could say anything further, and returned to the room.

"Everything all right?" Carla asked.

"I'll tell you later. How are we doing here?"

"I took the liberty of asking Les to check all the cameras available and to focus on the surroundings rather than the large group of pupils."

"And? Did you see anyone lingering, eyeing up the kids?"

"We've got one more camera to check but, so far, we haven't found anything that I would deem suspicious."

"Not what I wanted to hear," Sara muttered.

Les completed the task, and the three of them studied the area close to the car park of the school. He zoomed in, just in case there was a strange vehicle nestled amongst the employees' cars. Les took his time, even told them who some of the vehicles belonged to.

"Sorry, I'm not seeing anything out of place here either," Les announced.

"Not to worry. We know the abduction, if that's what we're dealing with, probably took place at the other end, in between Daniel saying goodbye to his friends and him walking the final few steps to his house. I think the next thing for us to do is carry out a house-to-house, see if the neighbours either heard or saw anything. If we can grab a copy, Les, we'll get out of your hair and return to the station to organise it."

"Coming right up. It won't take me long."

Fifteen minutes later, Les handed them the disc and then escorted them back through the warren of corridors to the main entrance.

Sara shook his hand. "Thanks for finding the time to deal with this for us, Les."

"Always a pleasure to be of assistance to the police, when possible. Good luck with your investigation."

"Thank you."

They made it halfway to the car before Sara's mobile rang again. "I'm getting pissed off with this ringing every five minutes. I wonder if I'd be within my rights to throw it in the river when we drive past."

Carla laughed. "I wouldn't, if I were you. It's not Todd again, is it?"

Sara stared at the screen at the unknown number. "No, it's not him. I can breathe a sigh of relief now." She pressed the Answer button and said, "DI Sara Ramsey, how can I help?"

"Have you found him yet?"

Sara frowned, not recognising the voice. "Sorry, who is this?"

"I'm Clive Moses. I've been told by Daniel's mother that my son has been reported missing. I believe you're the officer in charge of the investigation. I want to know what's going on before I drive down there."

"Oh, hello, Mr Moses. We're just leaving Daniel's school now. The investigation is still in its infancy. You're going to need to give us a little more time to get things underway."

"I'm coming down there. It's going to take me around five hours. I'll come straight to the police station to see you."

"I should be available; it depends on what occurs in the meantime. Drive carefully." Sara ended the call swiftly, not allowing him to come back at her. "Oh, great, now I've got two of them to deal with."

"Shit, I feel for you, but try to ignore them. Don't let them hamper the investigation, Sara. Promise me?"

"I promise. Come on, let's get back to the station. En route, can you give Jeff a call? Get him to arrange the house-to-house, it'll save me sending our guys out."

"On it now."

Sara didn't want to voice how she felt publicly, even to her partner, but inwardly she felt stifled, as if the walls were closing in on her. Todd had put her on edge from the moment she'd met him; her opinion of him hadn't altered. Now, judging by his abrupt tone, she was about to endure another showdown, this time with Daniel's father. Their interference was breaking her momentum, causing an unnecessary distraction.

"I said are you all right?" Carla nudged her. "And by the way, you just went through a red light back there. Lucky it wasn't at a main junction."

"What? I didn't. You're winding me up, aren't you?"

"I am. What's going on, Sara? I've never seen you as preoccupied as this during an investigation before."

"You noticed, eh? My mind is blown. Procedures that should come naturally to me seem to be missing the mark."

"You're allowing Todd to get to you, despite you swearing to me that he wouldn't."

Sara raised a hand. "Guilty as charged. I'm struggling to block him out. Believe me, I let rip when he rang earlier, and he was forced to apologise. But it's all right saying it, it hasn't prevented him from still hounding me this morning."

"You shouldn't allow him to get to you. Put a stop to it by getting Price to have a word."

"I think it'll come across as me being cowardly. In my position, I should have the guts to deal with his type."

"Ordinarily, I would agree with you, but you've had a hell of a lot going on at home that needs to be taken into consideration at this time."

"You know how much this job means to me."

"I do, which is why it would be in your best interests if Price jumps in and has an official word with him before things get any worse."

"That might solve the problem with Todd, but you heard what Isla Moses said about her former husband, and now he's on his way down here to hamper the investigation, as well."

"He might turn out to be a pussycat. Any parent, knowing that their child has gone missing, will be upset. We'd think they were odd if they didn't show any concern. You're going to need to sit him down and lay down the law, the minute he sets foot in the station. Maybe not go to that extent, but you know what I mean."

"Tell him where the land lies and ask him to have patience with me, us?"

"Exactly. Come on, I have every faith in you that you can do it, even if you're doubting yourself at the moment. Hey, consider this, have I ever got back in this car and said you shouldn't have handled a situation like that?"

"Er... let me think about that for a moment."

"Get lost. All right, for my sake, will you stop doubting yourself?"

"I'm trying."

"You're aware it could have a knock-on effect on the rest of the team, aren't you?"

Sara sighed. "Sorry, I should have realised but failed to see it."

"Do you want me to contact the hospital? See if Daniel was admitted overnight? He might have been knocked out cold and be suffering from amnesia."

"Yes, do that now, before we get back. Again, it's something I should have thought about following up earlier."

"Stop it. You had other priorities to deal with."

Sara turned and smiled. "Thanks, partner."

Carla placed the call, and Sara listened to the response from the receptionist on duty at the hospital via the speaker.

"Sorry, no unknown patients admitted last night. It was a quiet night all round."

"Never mind, it was worth a shot. Thanks for taking my call." Carla jabbed at the button on her phone. "Another waste of time. If only we had some form of lead to go on by now, but we've got nothing."

"Our only hope now is what the neighbours can tell us. We should hit the phones when we get back; hopefully Isla Moses will have sent me a text message with the numbers we need. You and I can go through the list, speak to the extended family of both kids and see what we can come up with."

"They've got to be together, haven't they? It's too much of a coincidence to have Sophie go missing and then Daniel two days later. Unless..."

"Go on," Sara urged.

"Unless we could be dealing with a copycat kidnapper. You know, prompted into action once he saw the press conference go out about Sophie."

"That's a bit of a stretch, even for you, Carla."

"I know, forget I said anything."

Sara grinned and said, "It's forgotten." She indicated left and drew into her parking space outside the station. "Let's see how we get on before Mr Moses descends upon us."

"Positive mental attitude, remember, all the way, not part of the way. You've got this, Sara. Let's face it, you've had worse cases than this to deal with over the years."

"You're right. Christ, I can't believe I keep saying that. I'm not sure if your head will fit through the door now."

"Charming. It will, I guarantee it."

THE AFTERNOON WAS SPENT CHASING their tails. Isla had indeed sent a text, listing the numbers of family and friends

Sara and her team needed to contact, but the response from all of them proved to be lacklustre at best. Depressingly, unearthing no extra leads for them to sink their teeth into. Sara had given Barry the task of analysing the footage they had brought back from the school but, yet again, nothing of interest showed up on the disc.

"This is driving me potty," Sara growled. "I don't think we've ever had a case where leads have evaded us for this long. What are we missing? Something has to be that obvious that we're all overlooking it. What the fuck is it?"

Carla and the rest of the team either shrugged or shook their heads.

"Well, I can't bloody see it," Carla grumbled. "Let's face it, we don't even know if the kids have been kidnapped or if they've packed a bag, without their parents knowing, and run off. We've tried to trace their phones; both mobiles have been switched off. We've actioned an alert for when, or if, they come back online. Other than that, I'm not sure what else we can do."

"Get Jeff on the phone for me. Let's see if anything has come from the house-to-house enquiries. There should be something back from the patrols by now, it's been well over four hours since the teams were sent out to the location."

Carla rang reception and handed Sara the phone. "Any news, Jeff?"

"Ah, yes, ma'am, I was about to give you a bell. I have Mr Moses in reception to see you."

"Okay, that's not exactly what I meant. Can you make him comfortable for me? Get him a drink after his long journey."

"Consider it done. I guess you were asking if there was any feedback from the patrols I sent out earlier this afternoon?"

"Correct. Any good?"

"Sadly not. The neighbours directly next door, well, one

of them, a Mrs Abbott, said she saw the lad come home, from her kitchen window, at around seven-thirty-five, but then she retired to the lounge which is at the front of the house. When asked if she'd seen anyone else hanging around outside the lad's property, she replied, no."

"Interesting. It's much lighter in the evenings now, so if there was anything suspicious going on then I suppose it would have been easily detected by anyone living in the neighbourhood. Yet another head scratcher for us to consider, one of many. Thanks, Jeff. I'll be down to see Mr Moses in a few minutes."

"Sorry the news wasn't better, ma'am," he said, his voice lowered, so that Clive Moses couldn't overhear their conversation.

Sara hung up and leaned her head back and let out a scream. "Give me strength. You probably got the gist of that. Again, nothing was gleaned from the neighbouring residents. I have to go, Clive Moses is here to see me."

"Do you want me to come with you?" Carla asked.

"Why not? Come on."

They made their way down the concrete staircase.

"How are you feeling?" Carla asked.

Sara faced her and grimaced. "Like he's going to wipe the floor with me, and I haven't got it in me to fight back."

Carla caught her arm, and they both stopped walking. "What? You can't face him if you're lacking in self-confidence, Sara."

"I know. I'm trying to get my heart rate to settle down, taking in some deep breaths, but it's not working, or should I say, it hasn't worked so far."

"You can't see him, not while you're in this state. Let me have a word with him instead."

"No, I can't ask you to do that. I'll be fine by the time we reach the bottom."

Carla pulled a face. "You won't, judging by what I'm seeing. Why put yourself through this torment when there are other options on the table, Sara? Please, let me take over?"

"I'm fine. Just having you beside me will give me the confidence I need to get through the meeting. Have faith, Carla."

"I do usually. But I can see you're tying yourself into knots, for what? It's not worth it. Without any major clues or information coming our way during the past few days, there's nothing we can do about it. You know as well as I do, that the second a clue comes to light, we'll be all over it."

"I know. Come on, we're wasting valuable time going over old ground here." Sara walked on ahead of her partner. When she reached the bottom, she turned to find Carla still in the same position, shaking her head in disbelief. "Are you coming or not?"

Carla's chest rose and fell. Sara could tell how angry she was, but she didn't have time to deal with that now. She had a possibly furious father to deal with.

"Are you coming?"

Her partner clenched her fists, shook them and let out a mini roar.

Sara had to suppress a giggle as Carla completed her descent to stand alongside her. "You win."

"I usually do. Stop worrying unnecessarily, or I'll keep quiet in future and refuse to divulge my true feelings when you ask the question. I'm a professional, most of the time. That means I can put on a show like the best actors in the business. Let's hope this time round I can give an Oscar-winning performance."

"So do I. If not, I'm sensing a touch of déjà vu, and he's likely tear you apart."

Sara inhaled one more large, deep breath, set a smile in place and fist bumped Carla. "I've got this, I promise."

She entered her security code into the keypad and opened the door. A quick glance around the area told her that Jeff had either relocated Mr Moses to an interview room or the room just off the reception area, where they had spoken with Isla Moses around eight hours before. "Where is he?"

Jeff pointed to the door closest to the main entrance. "In there. He's got a coffee to keep him company. Hopefully, it'll put him in a better mood."

Sara groaned and rolled her eyes. "As expected, here we go again. Okay, let's get this over with."

Carla followed Sara into the room.

"Hello, Mr Moses, or may I call you Clive?"

"If you want, and you are?"

"I'm DI Sara Ramsey, we spoke on the phone earlier. This is my partner, DS Carla Jameson."

Carla smiled, closed the door, and they both sat at the table, opposite the man who was in his forties. He was smartly dressed in a navy suit, although he'd removed his tie. He was clean-shaven, and his hair, though it was relatively short, was showing signs of age, with tufts of grey at the sides.

"Pleased to meet you both. Now, if you wouldn't mind going over the details of my son's disappearance with me, just in case my ex-wife missed something out, intentionally to keep me in the dark, I'd appreciate it. She has a tendency to be, how shall I say this? Ah yes, lenient with the truth. At least that used to be the case when we were married."

"And how long have you been divorced?"

"Coming up to five years now."

"Are you with someone else?"

"Yes, why? Does that concern you?"

Sara kept her smile fixed in position. "Not at all. May I

ask where you're now living, if it has taken you the best part of five hours to get here?"

"Sunderland, it's where my wife grew up."

"And how long have you been married?"

"We got married last year. I repeat, what does this have to do with my son going missing?"

"It might have a bearing on it. When was the last time you saw your son?"

"He came to the wedding. I drove all the way down here to pick him up the day before. We broke up our return journey by stopping off to see a concert in Sheffield. Got home with a couple of hours to spare the following day."

"Would you say you are close to Daniel?"

He fidgeted in his seat. "I admit, it hasn't always been the case. We're both trying to make the best of our relationship. His mother and I had what I suppose you would call a tempestuous relationship, hence the reason behind us getting divorced when Daniel was ten."

"Can I ask why you broke up?"

"Mainly because Isla thought more about her career than her family. To my knowledge, she still does." His eyes narrowed slightly.

Sara could tell he was struggling to keep his temper in check, especially when he spoke about his ex-wife.

"Sorry to hear that. How does Daniel feel about his mother's career?"

"He's accepted that she's never going to change. I've given him the option of coming to live with me and Lynne. I genuinely believe he's going to consider it in the future, but he's reluctant to move at this time, what with his exams being just around the corner."

"That's understandable. When was the last time you had any form of contact with Daniel?"

"I rang him at the weekend, on Saturday before my wife and I went out on a date night."

"And how did he sound to you?"

"Fine, like he normally did. You know what teenagers are like when it comes to speaking with their parents over the phone."

"Did you also speak with Isla?"

"Yes, but only briefly. The less I have to do with that woman the better. She's selfish to the core, always has been, I just didn't realise how much until she went back to work after Daniel was born."

"How much break did she have?"

"She waited until he was two. She breast-fed him up until that time and then announced she'd had enough of being at home with a crying baby all day long and that she needed to get her life back. We couldn't afford childcare, so I had no other option than to look for another job. My boss back then refused to let me reduce my hours at the office to work from home."

"What do you do for a living?"

"I'm an IT consultant. Of course, these days, because of Covid, the job opportunities in my field are plentiful, and most of the firms allow their staff to work from home. Living up north, I find there's less pressure on me. Life is so much more laid back up there, it's far less frantic than living in the south."

"When did the topic crop up? About Daniel possibly coming to live with you. Was that recently?"

He paused to contemplate his answer. "A few months ago, maybe around Easter. We agreed he was better off holding fire to complete his exams and then we'd knuckle down, begin the process of looking for further education opportunities up north, so he's nearer to us. He knows that he can move in with me and Lynne anytime. He's a clever boy, he realises what an extra pressure that might put on my marriage, though, therefore, he's reluctant to do it."

"But moving closer to you would mean that he would get to see you more than he does now, is that right?"

"Absolutely. I think you've asked enough questions about me. Now it's my turn. I need to know what you've discovered about Daniel going missing, and before you give me any copper bullshit, I prefer people to be open and honest with me. I'm also aware that the MP's daughter went missing at the beginning of the week, too. So, what the hell is going on, Inspector?"

Up until then, Clive Moses had been more than amenable, speaking about his son with pride and his ex-wife with the angst and hatred of any other ex-husband Sara had ever encountered. Now his tone was one of 'let's stop kidding ourselves and get to the facts'.

"I'm not going to lie to you, Clive, at this moment, we've got very little to go on."

He opened his mouth to object, but she silenced him with a raised hand.

"As with the ongoing case of Sophie Todd, we've yet to find any clues as to what has happened to either of the teenagers."

"Surely there must be CCTV cameras at your disposal, aren't there?"

"Yes, again, we've searched them thoroughly. We're currently going through the footage the school gave us from last night, where a vigil was held at the school before the pupils took it upon themselves to spread out and begin a search for Sophie. Daniel was involved. We were at the school earlier, before lunch, and spoke to two of his friends who were with him last night. The three of them walked home together, and they went their separate ways within a few feet of Daniel's home."

"Are you telling me my son arrived home last night and then went missing?"

"That's correct. We've also had patrols out there to conduct house-to-house enquiries with Isla's neighbours, and only one neighbour saw him enter the house."

"So he made it safely home? This is hard to take in. Isla said she arrived home after ten but neglected to check on him, to see if he was in his room. I couldn't believe my ears when she told me that. What parent isn't tempted to take a sneaky look-in on their kids when they've been out of the house for hours on end?"

"In fairness to her, Isla told us she didn't want to disturb him, which I can totally understand."

"Forgive me for saying this, but I can't. Have you sent SOCO into the house?"

"No, not yet. We... I..."

"You screwed up. Come on, Inspector, help me out here, that is what you're saying, isn't it? You took Isla's word for it and didn't investigate the possibility that my son might have been abducted from his home, while his mother was out at work, neglecting her child."

"I was going to say, that the information about Daniel arriving home... well, we didn't receive those details until just before lunch."

"Over five hours ago, and you've failed to do anything about it since."

"We've been working on other possibilities."

"Such as?"

Sara's gaze dropped to the table, and she twisted her hands together as she tried to think of a reasonable excuse to give him. Nothing materialised.

He could see she was struggling, and Carla didn't jump in to rescue her, either. He slammed his clenched fists on the table, causing both Sara and Carla to flinch.

"I demand to speak to your senior officer now. And no, I'm not leaving this station until I've seen him."

"It's a woman. DCI Price. She'll tell you the same as I have. I've brought her up to date on how the investigation is progressing."

"Bullshit. I demand to see her. Now."

Defeated, and with all her tact for coming up with probable excuses on the hop deserting her, she left the room to make the call.

"Sorry, Chief. I'm in reception with the father of the latest teenager to go missing. He's pretty angry and demanding to see my senior officer."

"That's unfortunate. Why? Have you done something wrong, Sara? Or is he just mouthing off, trying to undermine you?"

"The former. I think I might have screwed up, only because I've been intent on trying to figure out what's going on."

"You said the latest teenager. Are you referring to the MP's daughter?"

"Sadly not. This morning, we learned that another boy, a classmate of Sophie's, has also gone missing. It's been a hectic day. I've been here, there and everywhere... it's no excuse but... I'm sorry, it's all I've got right now. Would you mind coming down here and digging me out of this massive hole I appear to have slipped into?"

"For you, yes. We'll have a chat about this before we leave this evening. I'm on my way."

"Thanks, boss. Sorry for screwing up. It won't happen again." Before she returned to the room, Sara rang the lab and asked Lorraine for a favour. "Sorry, mate, I'm in deep shit and could do with your help." She recapped what had happened during the week and gave Lorraine Isla's phone number. "Can I leave it with you to arrange for SOCO to go over there, see if there is any sign of forced entry to the property? I feel sure, if there was, that Isla Moses would have told me when she came in to report her son missing. I know I've screwed up, big time. Can you help me out, mate?"

Lorraine sighed heavily. "This isn't like you, Sara, what's going on?"

"Pass. If I knew that I'd be doing everything in my power to rectify it. Please, can you help me, Lorraine?"

"I've got your back. Leave it with me. Good luck with the chief. And try to give yourself a break, Sara."

"I will, once this investigation is out of the way. Thanks, Lorraine, you're a good 'un."

"I am. When it suits."

Sara blew her a kiss down the phone and ended the call. She joined Carla and Moses who were both sitting in silence, staring at the wall.

"Well? Will she see me?" Clive asked.

"Yes, she's on her way down. I've also contacted the lab. They're going to get in touch with Isla, see if they can gain access to the property and check the windows and doors for any sign of forced entry."

"Forgive me jumping in here," Carla said, "But wouldn't Isla have already noticed if anything was amiss and told us when she visited the station to report the incident?"

"I believe she would have, but I still should have arranged SOCO's visit sooner, Mr Moses is right about that."

"I'm glad you admit you were in the wrong, Inspector."

There was a knock on the door.

"Come in," Sara called, relieved the chief had arrived, interrupting the tongue-lashing Moses looked like he had in mind for her.

"Ah, here you are. Inspector, can you make the introductions?"

Sara stood, offering DCI Price her seat, but she rejected it and remained standing. "DCI Price, this is Clive Moses, father of the teenager, Daniel Moses, who went missing last night."

"Pleased to meet you, sir. The inspector here informs me that you'd like a word with me. You've caught me at a convenient moment; I can spare you five minutes before I have to return to my office for an important call."

Clive's eyebrows shot up. "I'll be as brief as I can, if that's the case. I've been on the road for nearly five hours. I commenced my journey as soon as I spoke to the inspector earlier today, after my ex-wife told me that our son had gone missing last night."

"I see. Yes, I'm aware of the case. I take it you're unhappy about something that has happened during the investigation."

"Far from it, I'm unhappy about something which *hasn't* taken place that I believe should have been actioned immediately. I feel let down by the inspector and therefore believe she should be reprimanded by you and removed from the case."

"That decision isn't yours to make. If the inspector has overlooked a procedure during the course of her day, then I'm sure there must have been more important duties occupying her time. Unless you are privy to what events take place during an investigation, it is always hard for an outsider to understand the complexities of a case of this nature. Don't forget, Inspector Ramsey and her team have two cases running alongside each other, so, in the grand scheme of things, there are bound to be days when certain issues get overlooked. I don't see that as a mistake by the SIO, not when they are under pressure. Inspector Ramsey has been with West Mercia Police for over five years, and in that time, her record for solving cases has been impeccable. Her team has a success rate of ninety-eight percent, no mean feat, I'm sure you would agree."

Moses had the decency to bow his head in shame. He remained that way for a few moments and then slowly raised his head. He looked at Sara first, and then his gaze fell on the chief. "But she missed something I regard as integral to the investigation, if the True Crime programmes on TV are to be believed."

Sara opened her mouth to respond, but one look from the chief silenced her.

"And I'm sure the inspector would have realised her mistake soon enough."

"I would have. It's sorted now," Sara jumped in quickly before Moses could voice his opinion again.

"Only because I pulled you up on a mistake that should never have occurred in the first place," Moses added vehemently.

"As long as the mistake has now been corrected, I really don't see what the issue is here, do you, Mr Moses?" DCI Price stated.

"Not if it's now sorted. In my defence, all I'm trying to do is ensure that my son's disappearance is taken as seriously as the MP's daughter's."

Sara shook her head. "There's no question about it, Mr Moses. All the cases my team are instructed to investigate are treated equally, I can assure you."

"I can concur, Mr Moses. I'd have something to say about it if that wasn't happening. Now, is that all?" DCI Price glanced at her watch. "Only I have an important meeting I need to attend to with my superintendent."

His shoulders slumped in defeat. "Yes, we're done here. I apologise for going over the top. I'm sure you can imagine the turmoil I'm going through at this awful time."

"There's really no need for you to apologise. All you need to know going forward is that you have my best officer working for you. Please, allow her, and her experienced team, the time to gather the appropriate evidence, and I can guarantee you won't be disappointed. As I've already said, as a team, they have the best record in the area. They haven't achieved that by sitting on their backsides, twiddling their thumbs all day."

"Okay, you've convinced me."

Price raised her finger and said, "Of course, Inspector Ramsey will need the time and space to be allowed to investigate the two cases, without being interrupted by worried parents. She will update you periodically if, and when, something she regards as important surfaces."

"I will definitely do that," Sara confirmed. "I've never had a problem working with worried parents before. At the end of the day, I appreciate how difficult this time must be for everyone at the centre of this investigation. I have a few extra questions for you, if you have the time, Mr Moses?"

"I'm here now. I'll be around for the next few days, longer if my son isn't back in that time."

"I'm going to interrupt you there and make my exit," DCI Price said. "It was a pleasure meeting you, Mr Moses. Have faith in the inspector and her team. If you feel you need to speak to me in the future, my door is always open."

"I don't think that will happen but thank you for listening to my grievance."

DCI Price left the room.

Sara smiled at Clive and said, "Getting back to your son, can you recall him ever talking about Sophie Todd?"

He thought for a few moments and then shook his head. "No, I hadn't heard her name before I caught the press conference last night. Do you think they'll be together?"

"It's a possibility. As I keep saying, the clues and evidence are very thin on the ground at this stage, something we hope will change over the next day or two. Where will you be staying?"

"I'll find a hotel in town, probably the Premier Inn."

"Good choice." Sara handed him one of her business cards. "Ring me if Daniel makes contact with you, if you would?"

"Thank you. Will you ring me if you hear anything about either of the children?"

"I'll ring you if anything relating to Daniel shows up."

"Is the MP being a thorn in your side?"

Sara smiled and stood. "I couldn't possibly comment on that. We'll speak soon. There's no point in me telling you not to worry about your son, however, I want you to know that we won't let you down going forward."

"I hope not."

He followed Sara and Carla out of the room and shook their hands in the reception area, then left the building.

Sara let out a relieved sigh. "That was a tough one."

"Yes, but you handled it, and the chief also told him in no uncertain terms to trust us."

"She was great. I hope she meant it and didn't feel obligated to say what she did."

"She's got your back, Sara, we all have."

Time was marching on. It was almost six when they entered the incident room again. Sara was shocked to see DCI Price chatting with the team, as a group.

"Ah, there you are. How did the rest of your meeting go with Mr Moses?" Price asked.

Carla went back to her seat, and Sara came to a standstill in front of Carol Price.

"Thanks to you coming down to see him, I'd say he left the station in a better mood than the one he arrived in."

"I'd like a private word in your office before you leave. Have the team finished for the evening?"

"Yes, I was about to dismiss everyone. I'll sort out a to-do list when I get home tonight in readiness for what we need to tackle tomorrow."

"No, you won't, I have ten minutes spare, despite what I told Moses. We can go over the main priorities now, if that's okay with you? Unless Mark will be expecting you?"

"I can give him a call, let him know that I'll be delayed." Something in Price's tone made her stomach muscles clench, and she cast a sneaky glance in her partner's direction.

Carla's expression was one of dread, matching how Sara felt.

"You do that, and I'll send the team on their way."

Sara tore into the office and texted Carla. *Shit, I think she's going to sack me.*

Carla's response was instant. *Don't be so ridiculous. She told you downstairs that she wanted to have a word with you before you head home this evening. Stop getting so worked up. Relax. Ring me later, let me know how you got on.*

Will do. Thanks, partner.

Sara then called Mark's number. "Hi, it's me. Are you at home yet?" Judging by the noise she could hear in the background, she thought he was still at work.

"Not quite. I'm sterilising the equipment and getting ready to leave. What about you?"

"I shouldn't be long. The chief wants to have a quick word with me before I throw in the towel for the evening."

"Ah, is everything okay there?"

"Yes, of course it is. I shouldn't be too long."

"See you soon and, Sara, good luck."

"Don't worry, I shouldn't need it." She hung up and hoped that she'd sounded convincing, aware how astute her husband could be.

"Knock, knock, can I come in?"

Sara jumped at the sound of her boss's voice. "Sorry, I was

miles away. Yes, take a seat. I won't offer you a coffee, it's not a patch on the one you have at your disposal."

Carol sat. "Is that why you pay me a visit so often?"

Sara stared at her. "Do I? I hadn't noticed."

"I'm joking. Sit down, Sara, and stop looking as though I'm going to gobble you up for my supper."

Sara pulled her chair out, sat and smiled weakly. "Aren't you?"

"Hardly. I meant what I said downstairs. I'm not in the habit of lying, even if it is to save the skin of one of my inspectors. What did you miss? And why?"

Sara picked up a pen and began twiddling it through her fingers. "The problem occurred when Mrs Moses came into the station to see me this morning, to report her son missing. I wasn't aware at the time, neither of us was, that Daniel made it home last night. That information wasn't known until I spoke to his friends at the school before lunchtime. Around that time, I received another call from Mr Todd, wanting to know what was going on with his daughter's case. I'm not making excuses here, but after that call was finished, I went back to the man running the security footage of the vigil they held at the school for Sophie Todd. We spotted Daniel on the footage. I rushed that disc back here for my team to go through and organised a house-to-house for where Daniel lives. It honestly never occurred to me that Daniel might have been taken from *inside* his property."

"Okay, I can totally understand how you got caught up in things. Did Mrs Moses say if her house was ransacked when she got home?"

"No. She told me that she was tired and went straight to bed. In the morning, she called her son down for breakfast. When he didn't appear, she went looking for him, then she came directly to the station to report him missing. She didn't tell us anything was amiss at the property, whether she noticed it or not this morning, before she left the house. I should have still requested that SOCO do their thing at the residence, though, once I'd heard that Daniel had made it home. So, in that respect, Mr Moses had every right to be angry with me and to put in a complaint."

"Was it intentional?"

Sara dropped her pen and frowned. "Of course it wasn't, boss."

"Then I'm satisfied with your take on things. I know how much pressure Mr Todd has put you under the past couple of days. I thought we had an understanding that he promised he wasn't going to hinder you again. Do you want me to have another word with him? Would that help?"

"No, I think I managed to get the message across to him earlier when I told him that we are now searching for two missing teenagers."

"Fine, you only have to say the word and I'll warn him off if I need to. How are you coping with what's going on at home?"

"I'm fine with that. It's the investigation which is frustrating the hell out of us, as a team. The kids appear to have vanished. We know absolutely nothing about Sophie's disappearance, and what we do know about Daniel, not that there's much to know, has left us scratching our heads."

"In your gut, what do you believe has happened to them?"

"I honestly can't tell you. All we know is that the teenagers knew each other at school. Sometimes they hung around with each other, not often, though."

"Do you think there might have been more to their relationship? Could they have run off together?"

"You tell me. Had they disappeared at the same time, yes, I would probably have to agree with that theory, but they didn't. Sophie went missing on Monday evening and Daniel last night, two days between them. That's what I'm struggling to get my head around."

"Understandably. What background checks have you conducted?"

"The usual. Had we been only talking about Sophie, everything would have pointed to her possibly being abducted with the intent of getting something out of her father, whether that be financial or otherwise. Daniel going missing has definitely put a spanner in the works about that idea."

Carol ran her hand around her chin. "I agree. Had I been in charge of the case, I think I would have thought along those lines, too. I don't suppose your team have had a chance to do the relative background checks on the Moseses yet, have they?"

"Not fully. Mrs Moses is an accountant, and Mr Moses works as an IT consultant up in Sunderland."

"And they have no connection with Todd?"

"Not from what I can tell."

Carol's mouth turned downwards, and she shook her head. "I can see why the case is driving you to distraction, but I can't offer any further advice. What's your next step?"

"I'll have to go home and carefully consider where we go from here. I'm sorry you got dragged into this today."

"Don't be. I'm always here to support you, Sara, you need to remember that from time to time. Being an independent woman does have its drawbacks occasionally."

"I'll bear that in mind."

Carol stood and smiled at her. "Go home to your lovely husband. Send him my best wishes, won't you?"

"I will. Thanks, ma'am, for everything." Sara watched her boss leave her office and tipped back her head to look at the ceiling. "Where do we go from here?" she mumbled.

"You tell me," a voice said from the doorway.

Startled, Sara sat upright and glared at Carla. "You scared the shit out of me. I thought you left a while ago."

"I couldn't leave, I needed to know if I'd still be partnering you in the morning, or not."

"I thought you told me not to be so ridiculous regarding that?"

"It was a joke. Where's your sense of humour gone?"

"Vanished into thin air, apparently, like Sophie and Daniel."

"Aww... don't feel bad about this, Sara. We're doing our very best as a team, you're not alone in this."

"I know. Let's go home and start afresh tomorrow. Hopefully, we won't come into work to the news that another teenager has gone missing."

"Christ, there you go again, tempting fate."

They laughed and walked out of the office together.

CHAPTER 6

The evening before, Sara had found the time, while Mark was having a much-needed soak in the bath, to make copious notes of what the team should be delving into next as part of the investigation.

After she arrived at the station, she poured herself a coffee to assist her morning chore of dealing with the post. She was on a roll, and with minimal mail to deal with, she felt this was her lucky week. Then she called a meeting with the rest of the team. "Right, as you're aware, I'm guilty of screwing up on the Moses case yesterday; the less said about that the better. From now on, we're going to dig deeper than we've ever done during an investigation to make up for that mistake. Are you with me?"

"That's an unnecessary question for you to have to ask, Inspector," Christine replied.

"Thanks. You guys are great... the greatest according to what DCI Price told Mr Moses yesterday. Let's ensure we pull all our experience together and come up with a solution that will bring these two teenagers home. First of all, Barry, I know it's going to be an endless chore, but I still believe it's a route we need to tackle all the same. I want you to gather all the CCTV footage together and go over it, frame by frame. I think we need to concentrate on the Sophie case first because we're aware that Daniel made it home the night before last. Which reminds me, I need to chase up SOCO, see if they found anything untoward at the house."

"Will do, boss. I might need a hand, if I get overwhelmed."

"Give me a shout and I'll get Craig to join you. As it is, I need him for something else."

He gave her a thumbs-up.

"Craig, I'd like you and Christine to go through the system, see if there are any paedophile rings operating in the area which are currently under investigation. If there aren't, I need you to check how many paedophiles have been locked up in the last ten years or so, and if any have been released in the past month." She mulled over the length of time and corrected herself. "Make that the last couple of months. If that's what we're dealing with here, they're bound to have been on their best behaviour for a few weeks before getting up to mischief, if their rehabilitation wasn't up to scratch in prison."

"Leave it with us, boss," Craig said.

Christine nodded.

"Marissa and Jill, I want you to work together. Look into both families' backgrounds. We've already covered Todd's, but dig deeper."

"And what do you want me to do?" Carla asked.

"While I chase up SOCO, can you contact all the ports and airports? Issue the relevant alert for the kids."

Carla pulled a face.

"Something wrong?"

"I just feel we should have already had that in place."

"You're right, but there's no need to rub it in, partner. This is us starting over, from scratch. Addressing what we should have had in place from day one. I've had a long hard think overnight and I agree with Mr Todd, we haven't been giving it our all; that's not me having a pop at you guys, either. It's me being brave enough to admit that I might have taken my eye off the ball. But that's all going to change now."

"I don't think it's a case of that at all, but if that's what you want to believe, who am I to argue with you?"

"Just bear with me on this one. It's not like we've had any other leads to go on, is it?"

"True, okay, you've convinced me."

Sara smiled and went through to her office just in time to hear her phone ringing. "DI Sara Ramsey, how may I help?"

"Ah, Inspector, it's Ray Todd. I had a few spare minutes in my day and thought I would check in with you to see how things are progressing. No pressure on my part, I promise."

"Ah, Mr Todd. Yes, things are taking shape now. That's not to say we're any closer to finding your daughter but we're working on a few angles that we believe will bring some better results for us."

"That's a bit vague, Inspector. Such as?"

"I can't reveal any more at this time, sir. You're just going to have to trust me."

He sighed and added a tut for good measure. Sara closed her eyes, expecting a tirade of angry words to come her way. It didn't.

"Very well, it's clear that you're intent on leaving me in the dark. I promised you I would back off and allow you to proceed with the investigation your way, so I'll go now. Will you call me if there are any developments?"

"That goes without saying, sir. I know it's an old cliché, but I do believe it's fitting, occasionally: no news is good news."

"Yes, I've heard it said many a time, however, I've yet to

understand its true meaning. I hope you have a productive day, Inspector."

"Thank you, Mr Todd. Likewise. Bye for now." She ended the call and immediately rang the lab.

Lorraine, the local pathologist, happened to pick up the phone.

"Hey," Sara said, "I wasn't expecting to speak with you. What's going on?"

"I'm bored. Yes, you heard that right. I haven't had a PM to deal with for days and I'm finally up to date on all the cases I fell behind on. I take it you haven't had any dead bodies for me to deal with this week, either? I caught you on the news the other night, didn't I? A missing person case, wasn't it? Any luck there yet?"

"Nope, and now we've got another child gone missing from the same school."

"Damn. Any clues as to what might have happened to them?"

"None whatsoever. It's been beyond frustrating all week. The team are cracking on with things, but the more time we're spending on this, the less information seems to be coming our way, if you get what I mean?"

"I do. Missing person cases can be notoriously exasperating for the officer in charge. I suppose I'm telling you how to suck eggs here, but have you searched the local area, viewed the CCTV footage?"

"Yes, even the kids from their school were searching the streets, the day after Sophie went missing. That's when the second teenager, Daniel Moses, also went missing. Which reminds me, that's what I'm calling about, to see if SOCO has any news for me on the latest missing boy. His friends told me he should have made it home, but then his mother said when she checked on him the following morning, his bed hadn't been slept in."

"Ah, I haven't heard anything. I'll check and give you a call back in a few minutes."

"I need that information soon, Lorraine, so don't go getting distracted, you hear me?"

"Loud and clear, not that I would do such a thing. TTFN."

Sara ended the call and tackled some of her emails. True to her word, Lorraine rang back within five minutes.

"I can't believe you've stuck to your word," Sara said, a smile in her voice.

"Yeah, I wouldn't get too excited about that if I were you. The results are less than positive."

"Meaning?"

"I have nothing to share. No sign of forced entry. Everything was as it should have been at the house, in particular, in the boy's bedroom."

"Jesus, what the heck? Thanks for getting back to me, Lorraine."

"You're welcome. Sorry the news wasn't better. Let me know if we can do anything else at our end."

"I will. Thanks again. Speak soon."

"Look forward to it. And Sara?"

"What?"

"Keep your chin up. This is only one aspect to the investigation that hasn't come to anything. I'm sure something essential to the case will show up soon enough, it has to."

"I hope you're right."

Sara ended the call, completed her morning chore, and then rejoined the rest of the team who were hard at it on their computers. She walked towards Barry and asked, "How are you getting on with the footage?"

"Same old response, I'm afraid, boss: it's going to be a long slog."

"Hang in there. We've uncovered no end of possible leads via CCTV in the past."

"I know, but I can't help thinking this is going to be a waste of time."

She squeezed his shoulder and moved on to Craig and Christine. "Anything yet, guys?"

"I hate to tempt fate, but we've got a couple of hits so far, boss," Craig said.

Sara moved closer and read the notes he'd made.

"David Leech and Wayne Falkirk. I don't recognise their names. Can you give me a bit of background on each of them?" She pulled out a chair from one of the spare desks and sat close to Craig's.

"They worked together. Of course, they denied it all the way through the investigation and during the court case, but the evidence against them was overwhelming."

Sara winced. "Which was? Or shouldn't I ask?"

Craig's nose wrinkled. "It doesn't make for pleasant reading. Leech was in charge of kidnapping several children; their ages ranged between six and twelve. The kids were touted around the internet. I shouldn't have to fill in the details of what happened next, should I?"

"No, please don't. How were the kids eventually found?"

"A slip-up on Falkirk's part. He was caught on a sting operation, attempting to pick up one of the kids. It was an older child; she ran off before he could get his grubby hands on her. The area was surrounded by undercover cops, and they nailed the bastard. The evidence they needed to convict them both was all on their laptops. I remember hearing about the case through the station gossip. One of the officers dealing with the case had to take sick leave for a couple of months after he was tasked with viewing all the footage that eventually helped put them away."

"Sickening. Men like Falkirk and Leech should never be set free. It's not often I say that, but these people are a menace to society. They must have something missing in their brains, especially if they go after kids that young."

"I totally agree," Christine said. "Sickens the hell out of me. Taking a child's innocence in that terrible way makes me shudder. I have a friend who is also a copper down south, and they had to investigate a paedo ring working within a playgroup. She told me the images of what they'd uncovered, that were sold on the dark web for thousands of pounds, will live with her forever. Apparently, every time she tried to close her eyes at night the depraved images bombarded her from all angles. In the end, she had to visit the doctor, who prescribed her with a high-dosage sleeping tablet, the effects of which constantly made her drowsy during the day. Mistakes began happening at work, and she was forced to quit her job. The general public have no idea what we go through during an investigation, dealing with the scum in our society."

Sara placed a hand over Christine's. "I know, it's a thankless job we have most of the time. But looking on the bright side, we have to remember what a buzz we get from catching the bastards and making them pay for their sins."

"That's what keeps me going most days. There's no doubt about it, there are some days when we're all tempted to throw in the towel, aren't we?"

Sara nodded. "More days than I care to mention, until I sit back and consider the part we play in getting the likes of these people off our streets. At the moment, I wouldn't say it feels safer to walk our streets at night, but at least we're doing our best to work towards that aim."

Craig tutted. "Yeah, but sometimes it feels like the faster we put these fuckers away, the quicker a worse one pops up to take their place."

Sara nodded. "It does feel like that at times, Craig, you're right. Okay, so what's the upshot of what you're telling me? That these two men have been released, when?"

"One left prison two weeks ago, and the other, Falkirk, three weeks ago. I've got their parole officer's number here. Might be worth giving her a call."

"Let's put that aside for now. Keep searching, I feel sure you're going to uncover more."

"I already have," Christine said. "I've also got a Sidney Jackson, his name just flashed up on the screen as you joined us, boss. Can you give me a few minutes to check out his details?"

"Go for it. Give me a shout when you think you have it all, and we'll formulate a plan of how to proceed."

Sara moved around the room to where Marissa and Jill had their heads together. "Have you uncovered anything worth looking into further with either of the families, ladies?"

"Nothing, not really," Marissa said.

"I can't help thinking we keep going over old ground, the more we dig into their past," Jill added.

"Okay, I suppose it can feel like that sometimes, but experience tells us that it's a necessary evil and, should we fail to act upon it, it has a habit of coming back and biting us in the arse."

"Ain't that the truth?" Marissa said.

"That's why all this is a mystery and continues to baffle us. Why hasn't someone demanded a ransom before now, especially in Todd's case? I think that's what I'm struggling to get past. Someone in his position, wouldn't that be the first thing a kidnapper would think about?"

"You're not wrong," Jill agreed. "But what about Daniel's mother? I don't mean this to sound disrespectful, but she's a nobody in comparison. So, none of this is making any sense at all."

"But she must have money if she can afford to send her son to a private school. I'm thankful we didn't come in this morning to the news that yet another teenager had gone missing. I think, had that happened, I'd be teetering on the edge of insanity by now. What about the alerts, Carla?"

"All in place now. But if they were going to be shipped out of the country, would they really go by sea or air? They'd need a passport for a start, and they're older kids, it would be hard to keep them quiet. I'm guessing the kids would do their utmost to attract attention in order to help them to escape, or at least get noticed by the authorities. That's my take on it."

"You're right, I'm not suggesting you're not, but it's still something we needed to put in place and, yes, it should have been done immediately, not three days into the investigation," Sara confirmed. "I'm at fault on that one. So where should we be looking, then?"

"The ports are covered," Carla said, "So, even if there's a chance of them being shoved in the back of a truck, they'd still need to go through a port. What about if we issue some photos of the teenagers and get in touch with the local newsrooms, closest to each of the ports?"

"Yes, do it. Don't forget the Channel Tunnel, they'll need to be notified as well. I suppose I should consider calling another conference, give the press an update and let them know that we're now dealing with two missing teenagers." The idea gathered momentum, and she left the team soon after and returned to her office.

She picked up her phone and dialled the press officer, Jane Donaldson's, number. "Hi, Jane, it's DI Sara Ramsey after a favour."

"Hi, Sara, I bet I can guess what that is."

They both laughed.

127

"I'm clearly easy to read. Any chance we can call a conference for later today?"

"Really? I caught the one that went out in Ray Todd's office the other day. I take it he was guilty of arranging that one himself."

"He was, couldn't you tell? It was all over the place, not as well organised as the ones you're involved with."

"You know how to charm me. Carry on."

"Idiot. So, what are the chances for today then?"

"I don't see why not. I haven't got one planned as yet. Leave it with me, and I'll get back to you when I can."

"I'm not going anywhere. In the meantime, I'll be sitting on my hands to prevent myself from twiddling my thumbs."

"Are things that bad?"

"Yep, we're grappling around like pensioners stuck in a tornado. No leads or evidence coming our way on this one yet, hence me reaching out to the public again. The more we get the kids' photos out there the better."

"I agree. You need to keep bombarding the public with their details. It's worked for us in the past."

"Indeed. I'll leave it in your capable hands then." Sara ended the call then went back to the incident room and made everyone a cup of coffee. She delivered the drinks to the rest of the team and then sat next to Carla. "How do you think it's going today?"

"I believe the onus is on us now. That's not to say that what we've managed to do up until now wasn't good enough, so stop doubting yourself."

"I'm not. I feel far more confident about how things have gone today. Jane is sorting out another press conference for me."

"It can't hurt. To go out today?"

Sara took a sip from her coffee. "That's the plan. Making

the public aware that we now have two teenagers missing might make them sit up and take notice, because we've gathered zilch in the way of information from the one that was aired earlier this week."

"And whose fault was that? Todd's, right? It was a shambles compared to what Jane organises. He should have left it to the professionals to sort out. We're the experienced ones, not him."

"I suppose he thought he was doing the right thing at the time. He's used to being in front of the camera, but when it came to the crunch, he ended up looking like a duck swimming in the ocean with a shiver of sharks around him."

Carla pulled a face and asked, "Have you just made that up?"

"Nope, that's one of the collective nouns for sharks. I take it you didn't know that. Didn't you learn anything at school?"

Carla raised an eyebrow. "Definitely not shit like that. I can't help feeling like I've missed out in life."

Sara frowned until she realised her partner was pulling her leg. "Get away with you. I used to find it really interesting, learning facts like that at school. I had the best English teacher ever, Mr Miles. He was a very special man, all the kids loved him." Sara unexpectedly teared up and cleared her throat. "I kept in touch with him for a few years after I left school, but he sadly died two years into his retirement. His wife was devastated. They had so many plans they wanted to fulfil during their retirement."

"That is sad. Do you keep in touch with his wife?"

"Actually, when I remember, I send her a card now and again, with a message to say I'm thinking about her. She was so kind to me when Philip died. She heard about it on the news. Lots of people tried to visit me. I didn't want to see them, but the moment I heard that she was desperate to see me, I said yes right away. She entered my home, and we sat together and cried for almost an hour. God, hark at me, I'm off again."

"Do you ever think about him?"

"Philip?"

Carla nodded.

"Yes, sometimes, usually when I'm at my lowest ebb. Hard not to, we loved each other so much. That doesn't sound good, does it, considering I'm now married to Mark?"

"Don't be silly. It's not like you're cheating on Mark. Some people in this life can consider themselves lucky to find two soulmates."

"I suppose you're right. And how is married life treating you?"

Carla's gaze dropped to her mug, and she ran a finger around the rim. Sara sensed her partner was keeping something important from her.

"Carla? Shouldn't I have asked?"

"No, everything is fine. It's still early days, and we're both adjusting to our new roles."

Sara inclined her head. "New roles? That shouldn't be a problem, you were living together anyway." She got the impression that she should stop talking now, but curiosity got the better of her. "You would tell me if there was something wrong, wouldn't you?"

Carla nodded, and her eyes watered. "I'm sorry, I can't do this, not now. Not when I haven't figured things out for myself yet."

Sara leaned forward and whispered, "So there is something wrong?"

"Please, stop it." Carla propelled herself out of the chair, startling Sara. She tore out of the room and into the corridor.

The rest of the team stared at Carla's retreating back

then switched to look in Sara's direction. She shrugged. "Hey, don't ask me. One minute we were having an open discussion, the next she was taking off like a bat out of hell."

"Do you want me to go after her?" Jill asked.

"No, let's give her five minutes, then I'll check on her. Maybe it's the case getting to her." Sara knew that wasn't true, but she had to tell her team something to deflect their attention. The last thing Carla needed was everyone feeling sorry for her upon her return.

Her partner wasn't back after the five-minute limit she had set, so she went in search of Carla in the ladies'.

"Hey, Carla, are you okay?"

"I'm fine." She sniffled from inside one of the cubicles and blew her nose.

"Oh, hon, I didn't mean to upset you. Please come out and talk to me?"

"I can't, Sara. Leave me alone. I'd rather not talk about it."

Sara slapped a hand over her face and shook her head. *Not again! Please tell me she hasn't got involved with another bastard again, like that damn fireman. I can't believe it of Des. I set them up, for Christ's sake.*

"Carla, would you come out if I ordered you to?"

"I guess I would have to, what with you being my senior officer."

"Then I'm ordering you to come out and face me."

The door unlocked, and Carla exited the cubicle with her shoulders slumped. "Don't be nice to me, I couldn't take it."

"Of course I'm going to be nice to you, you're clearly upset about something. I'm your friend as well as your boss. Why can't or won't you tell me what's wrong with you?" She got closer and discreetly searched Carla's face for any bruising that had been camouflaged with makeup but couldn't see anything out of place. Then she checked her hands and her forearms, bare because of the top she was wearing and her lack of jacket, but still saw nothing.

Carla ran her hand under the tap and held her palm to her forehead.

"Do you have a fever? Are you coming down with something?"

All Carla's sudden silence was doing was making Sara more anxious.

"No, it's nothing like that. Please, don't push me, leave me alone." Then she was gone again.

Sara ran after her and caught hold of her arm before she entered the incident room. "I won't leave it. Either you tell me or I'll drag you up to the chief's office and she'll get it out of you."

Another moment's silence was followed by Carla gulping and then whispering, "I'm pregnant."

The news shocked Sara to her core. It was definitely something she hadn't considered. A bad health issue, cancer, needing a lengthy treatment had gone through her mind, but not this.

"Well, say something."

"I… umm… the truth is, I don't know what the heck to say because I don't want to put my foot in it. If you wanted a child, you'd be overjoyed about it, wouldn't you? Instead, I've just found you bawling your eyes out in the toilet and telling me to leave you alone. What am I missing here?"

Carla's gaze rose, and with teary eyes, she said, "I haven't told Des yet, I'm too scared to after… you know. I don't want to ruin things between us. It's too early for us to consider having a child. I'm too young for a start."

"Er, I beg to differ, you're over thirty, which, in my opinion, is an ideal time to have a baby. How do you think Des will take the news? Have you sat down and discussed having kids in the future?"

"Yes, but not yet. We talked about starting a family five years down the line, not after a couple of months of marriage. I've let us both down."

Sara grasped Carla's arms and gave her a gentle shake. "You've done nothing of the sort, accidents happen. I'm sure Des will understand that, once you sit him down and tell him. Yes, I did say sit him down first, before you divulge your status."

Carla shook her head. "Divulge my status? You've definitely got a way with words, Sara. But it wasn't planned, not yet, for either of us. What if he leaves me? Believes that I've tried to trap him?"

"Hardly, you're already married, so the latter is unlikely. I think you're blowing this up out of all proportion. This should be a joyous occasion, but look at you, you're standing here broken-hearted. Why? That's what I can't get my head around. Not unless this is about what has gone on in the past, with 'fireman Sam'. Is that it? Are you too scared to tell Des? Frightened of what his reaction is going to be because of what's gone on before?"

"Wouldn't you be?"

"I suppose so, although I probably wouldn't have put myself in that situation in the first place."

"Gee, thanks, just what I didn't want to hear."

"I'm sorry, it just slipped out. I didn't mean to say it."

"But you did, and now I know what you truly think of me... that I'm a coward who can't stand on her own two feet where men are concerned."

"That's effing bollocks, and you know it. Do you need to take some time off, to deal with this issue?" She winced when she realised what she'd said. "That came out the wrong way, and I apologise."

"I'm pregnant, it's not 'an issue' per se. Oh, forget I said anything. Let's get back to work."

"Not until you've calmed down. Getting all worked up like this isn't going to do the baby any good, either. Anyway, have you had the pregnancy confirmed by a doctor?"

Carla hadn't taken time off during the day lately. Maybe she had been fortunate to get an appointment during an evening surgery instead.

"No, I've missed a period."

"Is that it?"

"It's enough, isn't it? What does it usually mean?"

Sara rolled her eyes. "Search Google and see what comes up. I bet a month's wages that you get two dozen or more conditions it could be. Stress being a major one. Let's face it, you deal with stress day in and day out."

"Perhaps. Then there was that incident that happened at work for which I had to take a couple of months off to convalesce."

"Of course, that's it, without a doubt. Getting tossed in the air like a pancake on Shrove Tuesday will be the cause of it. You mark my words."

Carla's enthusiasm dipped again. "Except, I've had a couple of monthly cycles since then."

"You have? Hmm... well, that is perplexing then. How do you feel, in yourself?"

"Apart from getting a bit emotional, I feel fine."

Another telling sign of pregnancy. "My suggestion would be to stop off at the chemist on the way home and take a test, if only to put your mind at ease."

"Thanks, I think I'll do that. What happens if it turns out to be positive?"

"Then you and Des are going to need to sit down together and calmly discuss what to do next."

"That's the worrying part."

"It shouldn't be. Are you telling me you have doubts about him?"

Carla fell silent once more.

"Jesus, why did you marry him if you had any doubts?"

"Because I got swept up in the moment."

"Bloody hell, I've heard it all now. Had you been a giddy teenager, I would have accepted that reason without a second thought, but you're not. Answer me this, do you love him?"

Carla shrugged, and their eyes met. "I think so."

A shudder tickled its way up Sara's spine. "Give me strength, woman. I thought I knew you better than this. Why on earth didn't you put a stop to the wedding if you were having second thoughts?"

"Pass. Ask me a question I can answer."

"I've run out, for now. Can we revisit this conversation later, maybe after work?"

"Okay, you know how much I value your opinion."

"You do? That's debatable, especially with something as major as this, and I'm not talking about the possibility of you being pregnant either."

"Sorry, Sara. I truly am."

Sara cocked an eyebrow. "I think you'll find it's not me you should be apologising to."

"I know. There lies my dilemma."

"Get the result first and then deal with the other problem. If you are 'in the club' that could well be causing you a hormonal imbalance, toying with your emotions. Hey, I'm not a doctor and sometimes I talk a lot of shit, so don't listen to me, not about this subject. An issue I've steered clear from all my life." She added a chuckle just to ease the tension surrounding them.

"You're a top-notch friend, Sara, thank you for putting up with me. I know that can't have been easy over the years."

"Nonsense, a problem shared and all that."

The door opened, and Christine nearly barged into them

135

as she tore out of the room. "Oops, sorry, boss. Jane's on the phone, wanting to speak with you."

"I'll be right there, thanks."

Christine eyed them both warily and then returned to her desk.

Sara caught the door before it closed. She spotted the rest of the team watching them, some more discreetly than the others. "Try not to let it disrupt your work, you'll make the others suspect there is something wrong and will only encourage them to hound you for an answer."

"I'll try. Thanks for the chat, it's always reassuring to know you have my back."

"I would hope you would do the same for me if the tables were turned."

"Absolutely. Good luck with Jane."

Sara shot through the outer office and answered the phone on her desk. "Hi, Jane. Sorry to keep you, I was in the little girls' room."

"Needs must, eh, Inspector?"

"Exactly. Any news for me?"

"How does three this afternoon sound to you?"

"Sounds ideal. You're amazing, thanks for organising it so quickly."

"That's what I'm here for. A couple of the journalists asked me how the investigation was going. I told them they'd find out at the conference."

"Well done. Shall I meet you downstairs ten minutes beforehand, as usual?"

"Please do. I hope you have a productive day up until then."

"So far so good, I think." Sara laughed and ended the call. Then she sat at her desk for the next few moments to reflect on what kind of impact Carla's news could have on all of their futures.

"Can I come in?" Carla asked from the doorway.

"You know you don't have to ask. What's up?"

"I just wanted to say thank you for being you. An understanding and caring friend who never lets me down."

"Get out of here. I'm always here for you, hon, just remember that. Do what I said, get the proof before your imagination runs riot on you."

"I'll do it tonight."

"Ring me when you get the result."

"Are you sure Mark won't mind?"

"Why should he? This is between you and me, Carla. I have my own life to lead, and Mark has his. I wouldn't interfere if a friend of his needed his guidance at any time."

"Okay, silly me. Anyway, Christine has got the final paedo's details now if you want to come and speak with her?"

"I'll be right there." Sara opened her drawer, removed her packet of Nurofen and unscrewed her bottle of water to swallow a couple of tablets to ease the headache that was threatening to emerge. It was better to prevent one erupting rather than have to deal with the after-effects, she'd learnt her lesson long ago about that issue.

Christine proceeded to give her the lowdown on Sidney Jackson. "He didn't belong to a gang. He was caught surfing the dark web and kiddie porn sites on his laptop over a cup of coffee in his local café. A customer saw what he was doing as they were leaving and rang the police. He was a solicitor at the time, not your usual paedo, if there is such a thing."

"Yeah, we all know they walk amongst us. Some are more obvious than others, who get to disguise their filthy carry-ons behind closed doors. I've even heard of a few judges being caught out. That was in my previous position, up in Liverpool, not around here, but it would be foolish to dismiss that kind of thing didn't happen in this area as well."

"God, that's hard to believe, isn't it?" Christine shuddered.

"My take is, and don't shoot me for thinking this, his was a lesser charge than the other two. There's every chance Jackson has learnt his lesson, losing everything when he was put behind bars."

"If you say so," Carla chipped in. "I'm inclined to think otherwise."

"Go on, I'm listening," Sara replied.

"If he's sunk that low, to have lost everything he had to his name, where would he go when he came out?"

"That's what we need to find out. I bet he's sleeping on a friend's sofa or maybe holed up in a family member's spare bedroom."

"I'll check. I haven't got that far," Christine said. "By the way, he was released from prison two weeks ago."

"Then he's definitely a person of interest. Can you list all the names on the whiteboard for me Carla?"

Her partner left her chair, seemingly brighter than she was fifteen minutes before in the ladies' toilets.

Sara contemplated what to do next as she ran through the details of the other two ex-cons. "Any luck contacting their parole officer yet?"

"Yes, it's Tania Lance. At first, she was a bit off with me," Craig said. "That was until I explained the situation to her about Sophie and Daniel. She told me she appreciates how difficult it is to rehabilitate paedophiles in prison. It's so much harder these days because the numbers are rising year on year and there isn't enough staff to tackle the problem once they get inside."

"Great, so what's the answer? Burn the fuckers at the stake, just like witches were burnt, or women the authorities at the time believed were witches? Our society is so messed up right now. Is this the norm going forward? Dealing with kiddie fiddlers on a daily basis?" Sara's anger rose the more she thought it over. "Sorry, I went a little over the top there."

"Rightly so, I would say," Carla agreed.

"Okay, you were saying, Craig?" Sara prompted the constable.

"Tania told me that she had visited the men at their drab B and B several times since their release. From her experience, she doesn't believe either of them intends to reoffend in the future."

Sara crossed her arms and grumbled, "Ha, the stats tell a different story, don't they?"

"You've got that right, boss. Anyway, I asked her when she saw the men last. She told me at the end of last week."

"And the outcome of that meeting was?"

"She reported back to her supervisor there was no longer an issue with the men and less visits were the way forward."

"What? Remind me how long they've been out of prison for?"

"Two months and three months respectively," Craig filled in for her.

"As I mentioned earlier, what's to stop them coming out of prison, being on their best behaviour for a few weeks or months, or however long it takes to convince their parole officers that 'they're healed' and willing to live a normal life in society, then reverting back to the good old days?"

"It's messed up, I agree," Craig said. "Saying that, if the men are staying in a guesthouse, where would they take or keep the kids?"

Sara nodded as she mulled it over. "Which is why I think we should put them under surveillance. Let's face it, it's the only lead we have right now."

"I'd be up for it," Craig volunteered.

"I'm thinking we should put two teams on it, in case either one of them spots either of the cars and they split up. What do you think?"

"Sounds like a great idea to me," Carla stated.

"Craig, you pair up with Christine. Marissa, will you go with Barry?"

"Er... I'm up for it, but what about trawling through the CCTV footage, boss?"

"Carla and I can take over from you. I have to hang around the station this afternoon anyway because the conference is going out at three."

"With pleasure," Barry said, baring his white teeth in a cheesy grin.

Carla groaned. "Cheers, mate." She jabbed Barry playfully in the side.

"Boss, can I get her for assault?"

Sara frowned and shook her head. "You'd have to present a witness. I don't think anyone would be willing to step forward and back you on that count, Barry, sorry."

He muttered something indecipherable and collected his jacket from the back of his chair. The other three members of the team also got ready, and together they set off.

That left Jill, Carla and Sara to plod on with the background checks and scrolling through hours and hours of CCTV footage.

A little while later, Carla complained, "I'm bored already, and I've only been at it for half an hour."

"Stop whingeing and make yourself useful. I'd love a coffee."

"I don't need telling twice. Shame I haven't got time to nip out to the baker's for a sticky bun. I can't believe we missed lunch again."

"Shit, that wasn't intentional. I'll pop out and get some sandwiches for us all. Jill, will you contact the others? Tell them to grab something to eat en route. Otherwise, I'll feel bad if they're sitting out there undertaking surveillance with grumbling tummies."

Sara ran into the office, removed her purse from her handbag and asked, "What do you want, ladies?"

"Ham and tomato on white for me," Jill said. "I can pay for mine."

"No, you won't, this is on me. Carla?"

"Anything. You know what I like and what I don't like by now."

The phone rang in Sara's office. She dashed back to answer it. "DI Sara Ramsey, how may I help?"

"Inspector, this is Clive Moses. I was wondering how the investigation is going. I'm sitting in my hotel room going out of my mind with worry."

"It's progressing, Mr Moses. If something significant turns up, you'll be the first to know, I promise."

"What about insignificant? Has anything along those lines come up yet?"

Sara covered the mouthpiece with her left hand and sighed. "Not yet. I'll be in touch soon. Try to keep yourself occupied. Have you brought any work with you?"

"I've tried that. I'm too distracted and have difficulty knuckling down to the projects I'm working on. I just want my son back. I want all of this to be over. He needs to come home safely, Inspector, otherwise I won't be able to forgive myself for walking out on him and his mother."

"I can understand that, sir. Try not to worry too much. You have my assurances that we're doing our very best for you."

He blew out a breath and said a pitiful goodbye which touched Sara's heart. She and the team were doing all they could to bring Daniel home, he just needed to realise that. Wearily, she returned to sit alongside Carla.

"You look pissed off. Not because of me, I hope?"

"No, and I'm not, not really. Just sick to death of working

day in, day out, feeling frustrated. How are you doing with the footage?"

"Badly. I'm sure things will start to go our way soon, Sara, we just need to hang in there and think positively."

"Believe me, I'm trying. Bugger, I was on my way out to pick up some lunch for us. I'd forget my head if it wasn't screwed on."

"You're allowed to forget things occasionally, you know, no one is infallible."

CHAPTER 7

*B*efore Sara went downstairs for the press conference, she checked in with the surveillance teams to see if there was any movement at the guesthouse. All was quiet on that front. The news wasn't what Sara had been hoping for, but she had to keep reminding herself it was still early days with regard to the paedos.

"Hi there. Are you all right?" Jane asked the second she saw her in the ante-room.

"Yeah, don't worry about me. I'm a little anxious about how this is going to go. I'm relying heavily on what the public can tell us about Daniel and Sophie going missing. We just need a break to get the investigation going. This one is taking its toll on us at the moment, as a team."

"Can I ask what type of response you received from the last conference?"

Sara pulled a face. "Unbelievably bad. We didn't receive a single call."

"Hey, that wasn't down to you, that was more to do with how the conference was arranged. From what I saw of it, at home, the room looked cramped, not a relaxed atmosphere. Am I right?"

"You've got that spot on. As soon as I walked in there I regretted showing up. But Todd assured me he had everything in hand, and he was an old pro in front of the camera, so my hands were tied."

"It's all about creating the right atmosphere at conferences. The journalists need to feel comfortable and so do the viewers. That embarrassing event came across as chaotic. I'm guessing the people at home would have quickly lost interest in what was being said, especially with an MP running the show."

"I'd never thought about it like that, but you're right. Fortunately, he's the one who ended up with egg on his face, not me. The biggest regret is that it didn't help our cause in the slightest, and the week has been somewhat of a disappointment ever since."

"Sorry to hear that, Sara. I know how hard you work. Frankly, to have Todd disrespect you the way he did, leaves me speechless."

"I don't mind admitting that I've never had to deal with someone as arrogant as him before. It has been hard not allowing him to get to me."

"I can imagine, but he's in the wrong, not you. All you have to do is remember all the cases you've successfully solved over the years."

Sara smiled. "Thanks, I needed to hear that." She inhaled a large breath and added, "Shall we get this over and done with?"

"Can I give you a hug first, or would that start the waterworks off?"

Furiously shaking her head, Sara said, "No, don't come near me until afterwards."

Jane winked at her. "Fair enough. Come on, let's go."

The room was full of eager journalists. In one way, Sara was relieved by the level of attendance but, in another, her gut was telling her the journalists had it in for her. She knew she was being unreasonable but after the week she'd had she had trouble shifting that feeling.

AFTER THE CONFERENCE, Jane gave her a huge hug and with tears in her eyes, she praised Sara's contribution. "You were amazing up there. I don't mind telling you I had my doubts about whether you'd be able to pull it off, you sounded so negative before you went in there, but you nailed it. You had the journalists eating out of your hand. Even Matt behaved himself for a change."

"I noticed that. God, I couldn't have done this without you being up there with me. During the last conference my nerves were in tatters. Yes, it might have been because I had Todd sitting beside me running the show, but I think it was more likely to have been the fact that you weren't there alongside me."

Jane waved a hand in front of her. "Get away with you, it's because we're a great team. We feed off each other out there and get the job done."

Sara contemplated her suggestion and nodded. "I think you're right about that. Thanks again for making all this happen so quickly, Jane." She held her crossed fingers up. "Let's hope we get some results this time round."

"You will, I'm sure about it."

Sara returned to the incident room feeling more confident than she had all week.

"Dare I ask how it went?" Carla was the first to ask.

Sara beamed. "Actually, in spite of my reluctance, I have to say it went exceptionally well. We've done our part, now it's up to the public to do theirs. Jane reckons that, with the turnout we had, we should be on the right track this time and receive some valuable calls."

"Did the journalists give you a rough time?" Jill asked.

"I thought they were going to but, no, they were inquisitive instead of condemning, which was a bonus, considering Todd's daughter is still missing."

"Blimey, I genuinely thought they'd be gunning for you," Carla admitted.

"Me, too. Any news from the rest of the team, yet?"

"We've received one call from Barry. They're following Falkirk. He left the guesthouse alone about fifteen minutes ago."

"Is he on foot?"

"Yes. He might be staying local. The other team remained at the guesthouse in case Leech left the property. No news on that yet."

"Hmm... I wonder if they've spotted the cars and have come up with a plan to separate. It would be easier if this was all taking place in the dark, the teams would be less likely to be noticed."

"They're not stupid, they'll make sure the men don't see them," Carla said.

Sara had her doubts. Something was telling her it was too late for that and the paedos were on to them. "Okay, time is getting on. How far have we got at this end?"

Jill handed her a sheet of paper. On it was all the information she'd managed to collect about Jackson.

Sara speed-read the details. "I'm not getting any bad feelings about this guy. What about you?"

Jill shook her head. "I'm inclined to agree with you, boss. Compared to the other two, who have a cruel background, actually dealing with the kids they were after first hand, Jackson was 'only' looking at indecent pictures, he was never charged with laying a hand on a child."

"Yeah, I think we'll park his information to the side for now and concentrate all our efforts on Leech and Falkirk."

With that, the radio crackled into life. "Car eight to base."

"Go ahead, Craig," Jill replied.

"Leech is on the move now. He's set off on foot, heading in the same direction as Falkirk."

Sara stepped forward to respond. "Hold back, keep your distance from him. Keep us posted, Craig."

"Roger that."

Sara's heart rate doubled. "I need a coffee. What about you guys?"

"I wouldn't say no," Jill said. "Should we ring home, tell our partners not to expect us home too soon tonight?"

"Is Wayne on the road today?"

Jill's husband was an HGV driver, who was often away overnight.

"He is. Mum is looking after the kids for me. She can stay over, if necessary. She wouldn't mind, it'll give her a break from Dad."

Sara glanced at her watch. It was five-fifteen. "Let's give it another thirty minutes and then decide."

"Sounds good to me," Jill agreed.

Over the next half an hour, the teams radioed in with regular updates on both possible suspects' movements. One man headed into the city centre, and the other visited his local bookie, stayed there until five-thirty, before he returned to the guesthouse.

"Jill, you head off. There's no need for you to hang around."

"Are you sure? I don't mind."

"I'm sure. Carla, do you want to leave now as well?"

"I'm okay for twenty minutes or so, if you still want me to stay?"

"Either way is fine by me. I'm going to ring home, let

Mark know I might be late. I'm sensing not too late, though."
She dipped into her office to make the call. "Hi, it's only me.
How are you?"

"I'm at home. You'll be proud of me, I was a good boy and
left work early today. How is it going at your end?"

"We've got a couple of teams out on surveillance with two
people of interest being followed at the moment. I'd like to
see it through, if that's all right with you?"

"I'm fine with that. The casserole will take a while to
prepare and cook, so there's no rush."

"You could use the pressure cooker, at least it will cook
quicker, and you won't be hanging around for hours. I can
heat mine up when I get home if I'm delayed too long.
Although I can't see that happening."

"Good shout. I forget about that thing most nights. Will
you keep me informed?"

"I will. Speak later. Love you."

"Love you more."

She returned to the outer office to find Carla sitting at
her desk with her head in her hands. "Everything all right?"

"Yeah, I'm fine. My eyes were hurting from looking at all
this footage. No idea how Craig and Barry do it, hour upon
hour. They deserve a medal. The pictures are so grainy they
put an extra strain on the eyes."

"Forget about it. We've got plenty to be going on with for
now. Why don't you head home? Did you call the surgery?"

"They can't fit me in for a couple of weeks. I was tempted
to tell them to stick the appointment where the sun don't
shine but I thought better of it."

"It's getting worse trying to get an appointment to see a
doctor these days, isn't it?"

"You're not kidding. I'll stop off at the all-night chemist
on the way home and pick up a test. Hopefully, I'll be able to
do it without Des having a clue what's going on."

"I'll be thinking about you. Don't forget to give me a call later to tell me what the results are."

"If you're sure?"

"Absolutely, I'll be annoyed with you if you don't."

The radio crackled into life again, and Barry spoke. "Car seven to base."

"Yes, Barry. We're here," Sara answered.

"Falkirk is on his way back to the guesthouse after picking up two bags of shopping from the supermarket. I'm getting the impression there's nothing to see here, boss."

"Okay, Barry. Make sure he returns home and then get yourselves back here. I'll get in touch with Craig, tell him to do the same."

"Roger that."

Sara contacted the second team and gave them permission to return to base. "Go on, Carla, you get off now."

"I won't argue, I'm dead on my feet. Speak later."

"I'll be upset if you don't. Take care and try not to worry too much."

"Easier said than done. See you in the morning."

"I'll be here." Sara watched her partner collect her belongings and leave for the evening. The room felt suddenly cold and empty with only Sara being there. She shivered involuntarily and went through to her office. The view of the Brecon Beacons was covered by the low-lying clouds, and rain splattered the windows. "Great, I forgot to bring a coat with me." She sat at her desk and went over some paperwork she'd been meaning to tackle all week.

Around twenty minutes later, the rest of the team streamed into the outer office. Sara left what she was doing and joined them. "So, it turned out to be a waste of time then?" she asked.

"Looks that way," Christine replied. "Still, it was nice to

get out of the office for a few hours. Oops, I shouldn't have said that, should I?"

Everyone laughed.

"I'll forgive that slip of the tongue. Right, team, we've done our best today. Let's go home and get some rest. The conference went well by the way, thanks for asking," Sara ribbed them. "Hopefully we'll gather some decent information from it that will eventually lead us to finding the kids. See you all in the morning, usual time."

The team turned off the equipment on their relevant desks and wished her a good evening. Sara left a few minutes after and drove home. She couldn't help but wonder what kind of response they were going to receive from the public, once the conference aired.

WHEN SHE ARRIVED HOME, Mark was in the kitchen, clearing up. Misty was sitting at her bowl, waiting to be fed.

"I wasn't expecting to see you this early," he said. "Dinner should be ready in twenty minutes. How was your day?"

"Eventful. Is there any wine open in the fridge? Have you fed Misty, or is she trying it on?"

"Yes, some Chardonnay. I'll get you a glass, and no, she hasn't been fed yet. Anything new with the investigation?"

"Yes and no. Nothing we can really sink our teeth into as yet. I made a plea to the public today, the second one this week. I've got everything crossed that something will come of it when it airs later this evening." She opened the cupboard under the sink and removed a pouch of cat food and a handful of biscuits which she placed in Misty's bowl.

Misty purred and tucked in to her food right away.

"Go through to the lounge, see if you can catch it on the news. I'll bring your wine through. Fancy some nibbles?"

"I'd better not, it might put me off my dinner. How was your day?"

"The usual. I've had wee, poo and vomit aimed at me today, but you know what, I survived."

They laughed, and she stepped forward and kissed him.

"Eew... I can smell it."

"Maybe I should have showered as soon as I got home. I promise I washed my hands before I prepared the dinner."

"I was joking. Is there anything I can do while you're up there?"

"Nothing, go and rest. I'll be ten minutes. Here you are, take your wine with you."

Sara accepted the glass and went through to the lounge where she collapsed on the sofa. She scrambled across the cushions for the remote and turned on the local news. She managed to catch the end of the conference and couldn't help but think what a contrast it was to the one Todd had arranged. Sara leaned her head back and closed her eyes, hoping to catch forty winks before Mark came down from his shower.

She was out of luck, because the moment her eyes closed, her mobile rang. Carla's name flashed on her screen. "Hi, how did you get on?"

Carla remained silent for a few seconds. In that time, Sara's heart skipped several beats.

"It was negative, thank God."

"See, I told you that you were worrying unnecessarily. How do you feel about the result?"

"Overjoyed. I'm not ready to give up my career and become a mother just yet."

"I'd like to correct you there. Even if you were pregnant, there would be no need for you to hand in your notice."

"Umm... yeah, try telling Des that. He's got a different idea of what will happen once I fall pregnant."

"Really? Is he a caveman in his spare time?"

Carla sniggered. "I'll tell him you said that."

"You dare. Well, going back to what you told me earlier, you're going to need to have a serious think about where you go from here, Carla."

"I know. I'll think things through properly now my head is a lot clearer."

"Make sure you do. Don't forget, I'm always here for you. And I promise never to judge you or the decisions you need to make."

"I'll remind you of that in the coming weeks."

"I wouldn't, not about such a sensitive subject, I swear."

"We'll see. By the way, I've just caught the news. It was great. If nothing comes from this, then I'm not sure where we go from here, are you?"

"I was sitting here thinking the same. Let's hope we arrive to some good news in the morning."

"I'll be walking on air tomorrow, compared to how I've felt today," Carla said.

"I'll hold you to that. Being down in the dumps all the time has a devastating effect on your soul. I shouldn't need to tell you that after what you've already been through."

"I know. Thanks for the reminder, Mum."

"Go, enjoy the rest of your evening, you cheeky mare."

Mark entered the room as she was ending her call. "Everything all right?" he tilted his head and asked.

"Yes, it was Carla. Ringing up to tell me what she thought about the conference that has just gone out," Sara lied. She had no right telling her husband about the roller coaster of a ride Carla had been through during the day.

"Do you believe it will help?"

"I hope so. Want a hand with the dinner?"

"It should be ready to dish up now. You stay there, I'll sort it. Are you hungry?"

"Fairly. Not too much for me."

CHAPTER 8

*S*ara slept well the night before and drove to the station feeling much more positive than she'd felt all week.

Jeff smiled as she entered the main entrance. "Lovely day, ma'am." He pointed up at the sun blazing through the reception area.

"It is, Jeff. It's about time we had some decent weather for a change. Any news for me?" She could tell he had something up his sleeve by the twinkle evident in his eyes.

"I might have one or two leads for you and your team to chase up." He ducked down behind the counter, and when he stood upright, he held out a plastic wallet for Sara to take.

"Wow, I wasn't expecting this. You truly have made my day, and so early, too."

"Always happy to hear. I caught the news last night. I'm glad you've received some positive results this time, the last one was a disaster."

"I'm hoping what has come in leads us somewhere. This case has stretched my patience to the limit, so far."

Carla entered the reception area. "Good morning. Everything okay?" she asked warily, her gaze drifting from Jeff to Sara.

Sara held the plastic wallet up. "Good news in here, I'm hoping."

Carla raised an eyebrow. "Wow, if that's what I think it is, I'd say we're in for a good day."

"Possibly, we won't know that until we get started." Sara punched her code into the keypad, and the door clunked open. Once they were climbing the stairs and there was no one else around, she asked, "How's the head this morning?"

"Clearer, I think. Oh bugger, I don't know. I think it's going to take a while for me to sort out my feelings on this one."

"Let me reiterate, I'm always here for you and you're never alone. No matter how desperate you become."

"That's reassuring. Thanks, Sara. You're a true friend, I mean that."

"I'm glad you appreciate my caring nature." Sara laughed and pushed open the door to the incident room.

They were the first to arrive, although the rest of the team joined them within a few minutes. By that time, Sara had flicked through the notes regarding the calls that had come in overnight.

Carla appeared beside her and offered Sara her first cup of coffee for the day. "Anything new amongst that lot?"

"Hard to tell. A few vague sightings of Sophie we could check on."

"How vague?"

"Two callers believe they saw her on Monday night, one at an ATM in the city, and the other said they thought they saw Sophie on a bike, close to Huntington."

"Do you want to chase the callers up today?"

"I think we should make appointments and pay them both a visit."

Carla nodded. "What about Daniel, anything on him?"

Sara finished going through the final notes and sighed. "Nothing here as yet. Maybe something will come in later."

She gave the team a rough rundown on what the calls had consisted of and put the more interesting notes aside but didn't dismiss the others out of hand, not until they had investigated them further. "Take a couple each and make some calls, if you would? I know it's still quite early, but time is fast escaping us the longer the kids are missing. I'll be in my office for the foreseeable."

Sara took her coffee with her. She admired the view, which was totally clear today, for longer than she intended but was brought back to reality by the sound of the phone ringing.

"DI Sara Ramsey, how may I help?" Sara dreaded receiving calls first thing in the morning, especially this week, with two anxious fathers determined to ensure they remained at the forefront of her mind.

"Hello, DI Ramsey, I'm so sorry to call so early, I'm glad I've caught you in your office."

"Is that you, Mrs Cooke?"

"Oh dear, yes, it is. Excuse me for being so thoughtless."

Sara could tell there was something wrong the moment Mrs Cooke started talking. "Do you want to take a breath and tell me how I can help?"

"Umm... well... you see..."

"Mrs Cooke, has something happened?"

"I believe so. Oh, I do hope I'm not jumping the gun on this but..."

Sara closed her eyes and waited for the bombshell to drop. She was an expert at reading between the lines, and her thoughts were teetering over an abyss. "Has another pupil gone missing?"

"Yes, that's it. Goodness, I do hope I'm wrong about this."

"Do you want me to come over and see you?"

"Would you? I just don't know what to do."

"I'll be there in twenty minutes. Sit in your office and have a strong, sweet cup of tea. And no, that's not me being condescending, you sound as though you're in shock."

"I am. I've never had to deal with this sort of thing before. How do you cope?"

"It can be difficult at times, until I remind myself that if I don't act professionally the investigation will come to a complete standstill. We'll discuss things further when I get there. Do the parents know?"

"Not yet. I can't bring myself to tell the mother, that's why I decided to call you."

"Fair enough. Hang tight. I won't be long."

"I can't thank you enough, Inspector."

"You don't have to, it's part of the job. See you soon."

Sara hung up and immediately shot out of her chair and rushed out of the office. "Carla, we're going out. The head-mistress from the school is in full panic mode."

"Er, why?"

"Another pupil has gone missing. That's all I know for now, so don't ask me anything else." Sara left the outer office and raced down the concrete stairs.

Carla shouted behind her, "Wait for me."

"Get a move on."

"Bloody hell, I can't go any faster, I'll break my neck in these heels."

"When are you going to learn to wear more suitable shoes for work?"

"I'm thirty-one, not fifty-one, give me a break."

WHEN THEY ARRIVED at the school, they found Mrs Cooke pacing the top of the steps outside the main entrance. The

smile she gave was clearly one of relief and lit up her colourless cheeks. "I'm so glad you're here."

"Let's talk in your office in case we're overheard."

"Oh, yes, of course, you're right." She led the way, speedily
winding through the couple of corridors until she entered
her secretary's office. "Erin, put a hold on all my calls, and
could you bring us three cups of coffee, please?" she asked
her secretary without checking with the others if they
wanted a drink.

Erin nodded. "I'll bring them in shortly."

Mrs Cooke walked through the doorway to her office and
immediately threw open two of the large windows behind
her. "It's far too stuffy in here today. Still, we mustn't grum-
ble, we haven't had much of a summer so far, have we?"

"We haven't. Take a seat, Mrs Cooke, you look very on
edge," Sara ordered.

"I am. I know I keep repeating myself, but my oh my, I've
never, in all my years as head of this establishment, had to
deal with anything as upsetting as this. Three children now,
all missing from my school. You can't imagine what my
insides are doing at this time. I'm surprised I'm not
constantly running to the toilet to vomit. I have no idea how
I'm keeping my breakfast down."

"Try and take a couple of deep breaths." Sara breathed
with the headmistress. "In… and out…, in… and out. There,
is that better?"

Mrs Cooke ran a hand over her face. "Yes, that's much
better. Forgive me, but I think we need to tell Leona's mother
as soon as possible. I have her details here." She slid a piece of
A4 paper across the table towards Sara.

"First things first, her mother is bound to ask, how do
you know Leona has gone missing? If the news hasn't come
from her mother in the first place."

"I asked Mr Lawton to tell me if any children failed to

show up for school. Our attendance rates are exemplary, usually. He told me that he'd contacted all the form teachers between nine-ten and nine-fifteen to learn there are two children missing. One girl, Daisy Mills, was expected to be off this morning, she had an appointment at the hospital. However, Leona Fitz was definitely supposed to be attending school today."

"And you have a bad feeling about why she isn't here, which in turn is preventing you from contacting her mother."

"Yes, that's right. No message has been left on the school system saying that she's meant to be absent, and Leona's mum has never failed to phone in before. Which is why I'm unsure about ringing her and whether I'll be able to hold it together. My nerves have been jangling all week. I know how stupid that sounds, coming from a woman in my position, it's just that, after all that's happened to the others, the thought of three children now being reported missing from our school, well… it's really too much to bear. I don't mind telling you that I'm struggling to make any sense of it. I can't help thinking that, the parents will soon start blaming either me or a member of my staff for the children disappearing. I think that's why I'm a mess. Please forgive me if you believe I'm being downright cowardly about calling Mrs Fitz."

"You're worrying about nothing. Anyone with an ounce of decency can see how much you care about your pupils."

"I do. I wouldn't be in this privileged job if I didn't."

"I know. Okay, let me make the call."

There was a knock on the door.

"Come in, Erin," Mrs Cooke ordered.

The young secretary appeared and placed a tray, holding three cups and saucers, on the headmistress' desk then retreated quickly out of the room.

Sara smiled at Mrs Cooke, doing her best to put her at

ease when she saw how much the woman's hands were shaking as she distributed the cups. "Try and remain calm. There's every chance Mrs Fitz will want to speak with you once I apprise her of the situation."

"Oh no, I couldn't possibly. She'd probably think I'd turned into a blithering idiot if I spoke with her. Can't you make out I'm elsewhere in the school?"

"Leave it with me." Sara took a sip of her coffee and pulled a face at the lack of sugar.

"I'll do it." Carla jumped in and added a spoonful of sugar to both of their cups.

Sara inhaled a subtle breath to prepare herself and rang the number. "She works at the hospital as a manager?"

"That's right. An admin manager."

"And what about the father?" Sara asked as she listened to the available options the automated voice was telling her to choose from. She pressed number two and waited to be transferred.

"He's out of the picture. I don't think Mrs Fitz has had any contact with him in over ten years. Leona is a credit to her mother. She's a very bright girl and…"

Sara held her finger up as a human voice came on the line. "Ah, good morning. I'd like to speak with Mrs Fitz, if possible."

"Sorry, she's in an important staff meeting at present. Can I take a message?"

Sara rolled her eyes. "How long is she likely to be?"

"I'd say another ten minutes or so. May I ask who you are?" the officious-sounding secretary asked.

"I'm Detective Inspector Sara Ramsey. If you could get Mrs Fitz to call me on my mobile the second she becomes free, I'd appreciate it."

"Can I ask what it's concerning? She's bound to ask me."

"It's a personal matter, that's all you need to know."

"Very well. I'll pass on the message. Do you want to give me your number?"

Sara provided her with the details and then ended the call.

Now it was a waiting game. The more time that passed, the more anxious Mrs Cooke became. "Goodness me, I can't remember ever being this nervous, not even when I came for my interviews for this job."

"Have you been here long?"

"I'll be celebrating my twentieth year next April, if I don't get sacked by the board of governors in the meantime."

"You won't. I'm sure this is all a misunderstanding and it will be cleared up soon enough."

"Some misunderstanding, Inspector. Three children, all bright and caring pupils, may have been kidnapped, either immediately before or after school. In Daniel's case he was on a school assignment, if we can call it that. I still can't get my head around why neither of the families has received a ransom call as yet. Now we have a third girl to be worried about. I took the liberty of checking her attendance record as soon as I found out she was missing."

"And what did it tell you?"

"That Leona hasn't missed a single day of school in four years. She had an exemplary record, until today. I think I have a right to be concerned about her, don't you?"

"I do. All I'm asking is for you to remain positive, at least until I've managed to speak with her mother. This might turn out to be a simple mistake. Maybe Leona had a dentist's or doctor's appointment first thing and neglected to inform anyone."

"I can't see that happening." Mrs Cooke took a sip from her cup and replaced it on the saucer with a clatter when Sara's phone rang.

"This is her. Please remain quiet if you want me to pretend you're elsewhere."

"My lips are sealed." Mrs Cooke pulled an imaginary zip across her orange-coloured lips.

It was a similar shade to the one Sara's mother used to wear when she went to work. She had rarely worn make up in later life.

Sara smiled and answered her phone on the third ring. "Hello, DI Sara Ramsey, how may I help?"

"I'm Trisha Fitz. You rang me at work, left your number with my secretary and asked me to call you back. What can I do for you, Inspector?"

"Thanks for getting back to me so promptly. Umm... it's about your daughter, Leona."

"I only have the one child. Is she all right? Has she had an accident?"

"She's not been in an accident, not as far as we're aware. When was the last time you saw your daughter?"

"Last night. I left the house at six-thirty this morning without waking her. I had a very important meeting to attend here at work. It started at seven-thirty and has only just ended. Why do you want to know?"

"We're at the school. Leona hasn't shown up this morning. Can you think of a reason why she would be absent from school?"

"No. I can't believe what I'm hearing. Leona loves school. If you're insinuating that she's playing truant, I can assure you, she'd never entertain such a dreadful idea. She's aware that if you don't put in the work at an early age, opportunities are very limited once you leave full-time education."

"I see. Well, in that case, we believe your daughter has gone missing."

"What?" Mrs Fitz shrieked, almost bursting Sara's eardrum in the process.

"Please try and remain calm. Are you aware that two other children have also been reported missing from the same school this week?"

"Of course I am. I don't live in a bubble, Inspector. What are you saying? That you believe my daughter has been kidnapped?"

"That's a distinct possibility. I don't think this is a discussion we should be having over the phone, do you? Would it be better if I popped over to see you at the hospital, or would you rather come to the school?"

"Ordinarily, I would agree with you, but today isn't a good day for unplanned meetings, my schedule is rammed all day."

Sara stared at Carla and raised her eyebrows.

"What's wrong?" Carla mouthed.

Sara held up a finger to silence her and continued her conversation in such a way that her partner would understand what was being said on the other end. "I'm sorry if you can't work a way around your schedule even when your daughter is missing. Perhaps, when you get some free time, you wouldn't mind giving me a call back?"

"I'll do that. You need to get out there and find my daughter, not sit around with the head discussing what to do next."

"Thank you for your opinion on how I should be running my investigation. We'll do what's necessary to find your daughter." Sara jabbed her finger to end the call.

"What? Is that it?" Carla asked, clearly mortified.

Sara puffed out her cheeks and placed her phone on the desk beside her. "Wow, that wasn't what I expected at all."

Mrs Cooke put her hands on either side of her face. "If I hadn't been privy to that conversation, well, I don't think I would have believed it. I'm shocked by this outcome. Whatever is that woman thinking? Where do we go from here?"

Sara glanced at Carla. "I have to say I'm appalled by her

163

attitude, there's no way I can possibly leave it there. Whether Mrs Fitz is up to her neck in meetings or not, she will see us this morning. I think it's inexcusable that she should put her work before her daughter. How dare she? Sorry, I shouldn't have said that, not in front of you, Mrs Cooke. I shouldn't judge the woman, not from the only conversation I've had with her."

"I think you have every right to judge her if she's not prepared to drop everything after being told her daughter is absent from school," Mrs Cooke replied, clearly shaken up by the experience. "Maybe I was right to ask you to make the call, I don't think I would have taken that from her. I would have demanded that she left work and came to see me right away and I would have lost my temper if she had refused. What on earth is going on with these parents nowadays? I know the pressure everyone is under financially, but that burden shouldn't be detrimental to their relationship with their children. What the hell is this world coming to?"

Her speech got Sara thinking, but she wasn't about to reveal her thoughts here. Instead, Sara finished her drink and then asked Mrs Cooke, "Would it be possible for us to speak with Leona's best friend?"

"What an excellent idea. I'll get Erin to fetch Zoya now. The girls are totally inseparable." She left the office and returned to her seat a few moments later.

"Have you tried to call Leona? I take it you know her phone number?" Sara asked.

"Yes, we have all the children's phone numbers listed in their personal files. It was the first thing I did, but the phone was dead."

"Can I have it? We'll keep trying it throughout the day."

Mrs Cooke held her hand out for the sheet she'd already given to Sara and added Leona's number to the bottom of the page.

"Is there somewhere we can speak to Zoya in private? She might be reluctant to open up to us with you in the room."

"I agree. I'll sort something out for you now." She left the room again.

Sara noted the head had more colour in her cheeks than when they'd arrived.

Once she'd closed the door, Sara leaned in and said, "Maybe she's on to something."

Carla frowned. "What am I missing?"

"Maybe the kids were kidnapped by someone who thought they were being neglected by their parents."

Carla's eyes widened. "That's a bit of a wild assumption."

"Is it? All three kids come from single-parent homes. Not only that, but we've been led to believe the parents are all workaholics."

Carla scratched her head and sighed loudly. "Jesus, the more I think about it, hey, you could be on to something. How the hell are we going to get around this if that's true?"

"Get around it?"

"Telling the parents that they're probably to blame for their kids going missing."

"Shit, don't. I think we'll give that one a swerve for now until we've investigated the accuracy of my off-the-wall assumption."

"No, seriously, I think you might be right. Even if you are, it doesn't explain why someone would kidnap them or what their motive might be for removing the kids from their family homes."

"Maybe they intend to give them to families who have lost their kids, you know, who have died, and they want to make their families whole again."

Carla chewed her lip. "I think you should stop coming up with bizarre theories and stick to working with the facts as we know them."

165

"I've been trying to do that all week and look where it has got us. Nowhere. I know I'm thinking outside the box here, but it's all I have at the moment, and this theory is the only one that got my adrenaline pumping around my veins. I have to listen to my gut, you know that as well as I do."

"Okay, you've convinced me. Maybe we should hold fire on that for a few more minutes until we've spoken to Zoya. Perhaps the other friends we've spoken to know more than they're letting on about their friends going missing."

"That thought crossed my mind as well. I fear this investigation is still going to test us in the days ahead. I just hope we don't screw up along the way and end up fishing one of the kids' bodies out of the river."

"God, don't say that. I've gone all cold now." Carla shuddered, as if to emphasise her point.

The door opened, and Mrs Cooke joined them. "I'll show you to the room. It's different to the one you used the other day."

Sara and Carla followed the head down the first corridor and halfway down a second one. She came to a standstill outside a large classroom that wasn't in use.

"This should be adequate for your needs. It'll be in use in a couple of hours. You should be finished by then, shouldn't you?"

"Absolutely. We'll report back if Zoya has anything important to tell us."

"You will be gentle with her, won't you? She's what I would call a sensitive child."

"Don't worry, we're not in the habit of holding children down and forcing information out of them. Not that we do that with the adults we speak to, either. That's not to say we're not tempted at times."

"I can understand you feeling that way, especially after

166

witnessing the call you made to Mrs Fitz. I'll leave you to it. Zoya should be with you shortly."

"Thanks, we'll see you soon."

Sara paced the room until a slight knock sounded on the door. She rushed to open it and found a petite girl who looked about twelve, although Sara realised she must be older if she was Leona's best friend. "Hello, Zoya. Come in, please don't be scared. We just need to ask you a few questions about your friend, Leona. Take a seat."

They all sat around the large teacher's desk at the front of the room.

Zoya kept her head down and folded her arms. "What do you want to know?"

"When was the last time you spoke with Leona?"

"This morning. She rang me while she was walking to school."

"She had plans to come in today?" Sara asked.

"Yes, she loves being here. Always says she gets a feeling of contentment that is lacking at home."

"Can you explain why she would think that?"

Zoya's chin dropped to her chest, and she shuffled her feet. "I don't know."

"There must be a reason why she would think that way. Is she happy at home with her mother?"

"I think so."

"And yet it's here that she finds the happiness she is seeking. Can you see why I'm confused by that statement?"

"Not really. There are a bunch of us who feel the same way. That's why we never wag off school."

"Is that right? Do you know where Leona is?"

Zoya refused to look Sara in the eye and shook her head. "No, I don't. I hope someone hasn't kidnapped her like the others."

"Are you friends with Sophie and Daniel?"

167

"We're in the same class."

"That's not what I asked. Are you all friends?"

"Yes."

"Zoya, look at me."

At first the teenager refused to shift her gaze, and then after a few moments' pause, she glanced up. "What?"

"Do you know where all the teenagers are? What's really happened to your friends?"

"No. I don't. You can't accuse me of anything because I know nothing."

Sara raised her hand to calm the teenager. "I'm not accusing you of anything. All we're trying to do is get to the bottom of where Sophie, Daniel, and now, Leona have gone. Do you know something about their disappearance?"

"No. I've already told you I know nothing. Why do you keep asking me the same question, over and over?"

"I wasn't aware that I had, not repeatedly. You seem very fraught, anxious to me. Is there something you're not telling us, Zoya?"

"What the hell? My friends are missing, and you're here, hounding me as if I have something to do with this. I haven't!"

"I'm not hounding you. Believe me, you'd know it if that were the case. We're simply trying to work out why the teenagers, your good friends, have gone missing over the course of this week. Please, won't you help us? We're very concerned about their safety now, especially Sophie, who has been missing the longest."

"I know nothing. We held a vigil for Sophie on Tuesday, why would we do that if...?"

"If you knew where she was, is that what you were about to say?"

"Yes. See, you're hounding me for answers that I don't have. I'm here to assist you with your enquiries. I'm doing my best, I'm nervous talking to a police officer, you're not taking that into consideration. Instead, here you are, in my face, badgering me for answers."

Sara and Carla glanced at each other and frowned.

"You keep using the words *hounding* and *badgering* as if I'm torturing you into telling me where your friends are. If you know something, it would be better if you tell me now, otherwise I will have no alternative but to take you in for questioning. Your parents will also be sent for before I interview you, is that what you want, Zoya?"

"No, my mother is very busy, she'd kill me if you interrupted her at work."

"I doubt if that would be the case. It's not my intention to be heavy-handed with witnesses, not unless they give me the impression that they know more than they're letting on."

"I don't, I promise. Can I go now?"

Again, Zoya refused to make eye contact with either Sara or Carla, casting a huge cloud over whether she was telling the truth or not. Sara summed the situation up quickly and came to the conclusion that she was indeed going to need to get heavy-handed with the teenager if they were going to learn the truth.

"Okay, here's the deal, you have five minutes to break your silence on this matter or we'll relocate to the police station to continue this conversation in an interview room with your mother and her solicitor present. The choice is yours, Zoya."

The teenager put her hands over her face and sobbed.

Sara touched her arm. "Zoya, I appreciate how difficult this must be for you, especially if you've been sworn to secrecy. Have you?"

Zoya dropped her hands and, as well as the tears glistening on her cheeks, more tears welled up, ready to replace the ones she had swiped away with the back of her hand. "I don't know what you mean."

Sara raised her eyebrows. "Don't kid a kidder. We know there's more to this story than we've managed to uncover during the week. What is it?"

"I don't know what you're talking about."

Sara stood. Carla closed her notebook and followed suit.

Zoya's gaze shifted between them. "Are you going now?"

"Yes, we're going back to the station, and you're coming with us. You can call your mother en route, tell her to meet us there."

"No, please," Zoya shouted. "Don't make me do this. It isn't fair for you to pick on me like this. I haven't done anything wrong."

Sara shrugged. "I gave you a choice, and you opted not to confide in us. We're experienced enough to realise when someone is lying to us, or should I say evading the truth? If your friends are in danger you need to tell us, now."

"They're not. That's all I know."

Sara took her seat again and through narrowed eyes, she asked, "How do you know they're not in danger? Have they been kidnapped?"

Zoya shook her head. "I can't tell you. They'd turn their backs on me if I told you."

"Reading between the lines, are you telling us that your friends have run away together?" Her question was ignored by the distraught teenager, so Sara repeated it. "Zoya, have they run away together?"

Zoya sobbed again, but through her tears she gave a brief nod.

"Was that a yes?"

The teenager wiped her snotty nose on the sleeve of her jumper. "I'm sorry. This has been a nightmare for me."

"May I ask why?"

"Because I wasn't meant to know. I overheard Sophie, Daniel and Leona whispering about it one day. They warned me not to say anything. They know it's impossible for me to keep a secret, they're always telling me I have the biggest mouth and should try keeping it shut once in a while. They upset me when they have a go at me."

"Can you tell us what you overheard them talking about?"

"It wasn't much. I'm not just saying that."

"Just tell us what they said. You want us to find them, don't you? Before something serious happens to them."

"It won't. They said that everything had been well planned and no one would find them."

"But do you know where they are?"

"Not really. I only know they're together."

Sara's impatience was getting the better of her. Zoya was determined to make them work for the information they needed to get the investigation solved. "Still in Hereford, or are they meeting up and heading elsewhere?"

"I don't know. That's all I overheard. I swear it is. Please don't tell Mrs Cooke I've told you this, she'd probably give me detention for a month if she finds out. She'll blame me for not coming forward and telling the truth."

"What about Nadine and Amy, do they know about the plan?"

Again, she refused to look up at Sara. "I don't know, you'll have to ask them."

"We'll do that now."

"No... you can't do that, they'll think I've dropped them in it."

"Okay, we'll revisit that another time. We need to get going, there's somewhere else we need to be. Thank you for finally having the courage to speak with us. I'll give you one of my cards. Please ring me if you hear where they might be. We're worried about them, and so are their families."

"I doubt if that's the case."

"Are the kids feeling neglected? Is that why they've run away? To teach their parents a lesson?"

"You knew?"

"We came to that conclusion not long ago but haven't had the chance to act upon it yet."

"Do their families know?"

"Not yet. Do you think it will come as a shock to them once they learn the truth?" Sara asked.

Zoya fidgeted in her seat under Sara's scrutinising gaze. "Yes. They're all selfish. That's what Sophie, Daniel and Leona think. Their parents are rarely home; my friends usually have to fend for themselves. Sophie told us her father eats out most nights and expects her to cook her own meals when she gets home from school. That can't be right, can it? I can't imagine going home at night and Mum not being there."

"Are both your parents at home?"

"Yes. I know I'm lucky in that respect. But Mum and Dad still argue most days. I wouldn't say our family is happy. I tried to tell the others that they were well off in that respect, but they refused to listen to me. Told me I talk a lot of nonsense and that I should keep my nose out of their business."

"That's a bit unfair, isn't it? So, they don't allow you to voice your own opinion?"

"It does seem that way. They have hurt my feelings a lot lately, keeping secrets from me. The conversation always stops when I get close to them as well, which really gets on my nerves."

"Maybe you should rethink being friends with them if they continue to treat you that way."

"Oh no. Most of the time they're right. I enjoy hanging around with them. They're a lot of fun to be with."

"Well, that's up to you. Thank you for what you've told us here today. You can go back to your class now."

"I hope you find them soon."

"So do we, because if they're intentionally hiding out somewhere and haven't been kidnapped, they've been successful in keeping us away from our 'real police work', putting other peoples' lives at risk. That's an added fact they should be proud of as a group." Sara struggled to keep the anger from her tone.

Zoya stood and walked away from them. At the door, she turned and uttered a faint apology, then left the room.

Sara rose from her seat and lashed out at the back of the chair. "Can you effing believe that? Come on, let's get out of here. I'll ring Mrs Cooke from the car once I've calmed down a bit."

Carla fell quiet and followed her out of the room and up the corridor to the main entrance. Outside, she said, "You're going to need to take a couple of breaths and calm down before I get in the car with you, Sara."

"You reckon? If there's one thing I despise most in this job it's being taken for a fool."

"Playing devil's advocate here, maybe Zoya has got this all wrong. Perhaps she's just a bitter and twisted little girl, set on revenge." Carla walked away from her, towards the car.

Sara caught up and pulled on Carla's arm. "What's going on?"

"This isn't like you. Taking someone's word for it without the evidence to back up what they're saying."

"At any other time, on any other case, I would agree with you, but something hasn't sat well with me all week, you know that. What if this is the cause of that uncertainty?"

"I think we should hold back from criticising the kids too much until they've been found, just in case."

"I don't agree with you. They're coming across like a

bunch of spoilt private school kids, and I can't wait until I get my ruddy hands on them."

They continued their walk towards the car. Sara opened it, and they jumped in. There, she sat for a moment, considering what to do next. She lashed out at the steering wheel and switched on the engine.

"Where are we going?"

"To the hospital. To visit Leona's mother."

"Uh-oh, I sense you're going there to give her a piece of your mind."

"And what if I am?"

"Don't do it, Sara, you're better than that. Don't mess things up now. You can tell the parents what you think of them once we've found the kids and they reveal the truth. Saying something now will only result in one thing—you probably getting the sack."

Sara tipped her head back and growled like a caged animal, desperately searching for a means of escaping. "I know you're right but…"

"No buts. Let's carry on with the investigation, as if the conversation with Zoya hadn't happened."

"I can't do that, knowing that the three teenagers are holed up in a house somewhere, sodding laughing at us."

Carla shook her head. "You're wrong, Sara. Once you've cooled down enough, you'll realise this has nothing to do with them intentionally wasting police time. I think it has more to do with them making a stand, a rightful stand against their parents."

Sara didn't get a chance to answer because her mobile rang. "Shit! It's Todd. What the fuck am I going to tell him?"

"The usual. Act dumb for now. If you have to, tell him you're too busy to talk as another teenager has gone missing, that should keep him off your back for a while."

"You're right. I need to get out of the car, swallow down

some fresh air before I speak to him." She pushed open the door and sucked in a calming lungful. "DI Sara Ramsey, what can I do for you, Mr Todd?"

"Oh, you are at work, after all. I was under the impression, with you not answering the phone, you were still at home."

"Hardly. Can you make this quick? I'm up to my eyes in it here."

"Umm... okay. I was contacting you to see how the investigation was going."

"It's going. I have no further update for you at this time. Now, if you'll excuse me, I have an important meeting to attend with a parent."

"About what?"

"Actually, that's none of your business, but I'm going to tell you anyway. First thing this morning, another teenager was reported missing by the headmistress of the school, the same school your daughter and Daniel Moses attend."

"What? And you don't think that kind of news concerns me?"

"Not directly, no. Now if you don't mind, I have to get on and let the parents know about their child's disappearance."

"Of course. Yes, they'll probably be going out of their minds with worry, like I am."

"More than likely. I won't know until I meet them, or should I say her, the mother. Like you, Mrs Fitz is raising her child on her own."

"I assure you, it can be a thankless task most of the time, Inspector."

"I'll have to take your word for that, sir. I'll be in touch soon, should any information regarding your daughter come my way."

"Thank you."

Sara's tone had been clipped and professional throughout, it had to be to get her message across. She ended the call and got back into the car.

"How did it go?"

"The same as usual, except I was blunt and to the point with him, more than I've ever been."

"And what was his reaction to that?"

Sara started the engine. "To be honest with you, I couldn't give a toss. Let's get on the road, and then I'll give Mrs Cooke an update. I'm not one for breaking my promises."

"No, you're the fairest person I know."

"Thanks." Sara punched in her passcode and handed Carla the phone. "Scroll back to the first call I received this morning, at around nine-twenty, and dial that number for me, will you?"

"Consider it done."

The phone rang, and Erin, the secretary, answered the call. "It's DI Ramsey. Is it convenient to speak with Mrs Cooke, please, Erin?"

"Yes, I think so. I'll pass you through."

There was a moment's silence before Mrs Cooke came on the line. "Hello, Inspector. How did you get on with Zoya?"

"Eventually she opened up to us. To be honest with you, I'm still trying to digest what she told us."

"Oh, may I ask why?"

"It's too complicated to tell you over the phone. Suffice to say, we don't believe the children are in imminent danger, that's the impression we got from speaking with Zoya."

"Really? Can't you tell me more than that?"

"Briefly." She explained what had happened with Nadine and Amy earlier. "I'm sorry, I need to keep the line clear now, Mrs Cooke. I'll be in touch with you again soon, unless anything else happens at your end that you think I should know about."

"Yes, yes, I'll contact you if anything else comes to light.

Thank you for coming out to see me today. I hope you can forgive me for being in such a mess when you got here."

"Don't mention it. We all get days like that. Take care."

"Good luck with your investigation and thank you for being so understanding."

"Not a problem. Speak soon, Mrs Cooke." Sara ran a finger over her throat, telling Carla to cut the call.

"There, that wasn't too bad, was it?"

"For you maybe. God, this week has been one of the worst I've had to deal with in my time on the Force, and to think a bunch of teenagers are to blame. Shame on them."

"Yeah, they don't realise what trouble they've put everyone through this week, most of all their parents. Which was their intention, after all."

"Kids, who'd have them, eh?"

Carla sniggered. "Who indeed, when they can wind you up like a coiled spring most of the time? We still need to locate the buggers."

"You're not wrong, and when we do…"

CHAPTER 9

*S*ara and Carla arrived at the hospital and rode the lift up to the third floor where the management offices were located. Sara flashed her ID at the receptionist and asked to speak with Mrs Fitz.

"I'm sorry, I'm afraid that won't be possible. She has an extremely busy schedule all day, meeting after meeting. You'll have to come back tomorrow to see her."

"No, that's not possible. We're here to see her now. I'm sure she'll agree to see us once she knows we're on the premises."

"This is most inappropriate. I don't believe you have any authority over the staff in this building."

"I think you'll find you're wrong when we're investigating an important crime."

The receptionist's cheeks flared to a crimson. "I…"

"Just get Mrs Fitz out here, now," Sara shouted, sick of the shit people were flinging at her when all she was seeking to do was her job.

The receptionist tearfully mumbled an apology and made the call with her back turned to them. "Yes, I've tried to tell them that... I'm sorry... I believe it would be better if you came and spoke to them yourself... Thank you." She swivelled in her chair and offered up the weakest of smiles. "She'll be right out. She's not happy about the situation, though."

"That's tough. We wouldn't be inconveniencing her if it wasn't important."

They stepped away from the desk but chose not to take a seat.

A woman in her forties, in a bright-orange suit, came hurtling down the corridor to meet them. "Are you the woman I spoke to on the phone earlier?"

"I'm Detective Inspector Ramsey, that's correct. Is there somewhere private we can hold this conversation?"

Seething, the woman pointed at a room behind Sara. "In there. You'd better make this quick. I told you earlier how busy my schedule is today."

"You did, but as I informed you, your daughter has been reported missing. To any other parent, that atrocious news would take precedence over a bunch of meetings."

Mrs Fitz glared, huffed out a breath and led the way into the room. "How dare you come here and speak to me like that?"

"Like what? All I've done so far is tell you the truth. Aren't you concerned about your daughter's well-being?"

"What type of person do you take me for?"

She didn't offer them a seat. She stood there, her foot tapping in her three-inch patent black heels, with her arms firmly crossed.

"I'm not sure, is the honest answer. I just assumed that you would be more worried about your daughter. To be honest with you, I'm struggling to see why her disappearance isn't a major concern to you at this time."

"Because, if you must know, I have a huge deal on the table, and if the matter isn't dealt with appropriately today, my team and I could be down the job centre tomorrow. Is that clear enough for you, Inspector?"

"Not really. Do you often place your career over the welfare of your child?"

"How dare you?" She took a step forward and raised her hand, ready to strike Sara's face.

Sara's reaction was as swift as the woman trying to attack her. She caught Mrs Fitz's wrist and twisted it. "I wouldn't do that if I were you, not unless you want me to arrest you for assaulting a police officer. Do you? Or don't you have time for that in your busy schedule either?"

Mrs Fitz yanked her arm out of Sara's hand. "I'm sorry. You have no idea the pressure I'm under. If I don't turn things around today..."

"Yes, you've already told us what it will lead to. But that's not my problem. Your daughter going missing, however, that's a different story entirely."

Mrs Fitz recoiled and walked backwards towards the chairs sitting along the wall and flopped into one of them. She placed her head in her hands and cried.

It was the last thing Sara expected, coming from someone who had portrayed herself, up until then, as a hard bitch. Sara sat in the chair beside her and tentatively placed an arm around her shoulder. She expected the woman to shrug her off. She didn't.

"I'm sorry. I don't know what has got into me lately. I've been overwhelmed by the amount of pressure the board is putting me under. I felt I had to devote all the hours I had spare in the day to my career and, in the process, I'm guilty of neglecting my daughter. Do you know what has happened to her? How can I help?"

Sara explained the position they found themselves in, aware that the children might be hiding somewhere to make their parents suffer.

"Oh God, yes, that does sound plausible, doesn't it? But why didn't Leona try to speak to me about how she felt? Why would she go to such extremes to get her point across?"

"Maybe she has tried speaking to you over the past few months. If you admit you've been overwhelmed with work lately, perhaps you weren't really paying her attention when she spoke."

Mrs Fitz nodded. "Yes, I think you might be right. I'm sorry, it should never have come to this, my daughter deserved to be treated better. What can I do to make it right?"

"That's the sixty-four-million-dollar question, one I'm not sure I can answer as yet. Unless you can tell us where she and her friends are likely to be hiding?"

She immediately started shaking her head. "No, I can't think of a single place. I'm sorry. I wish I knew. I want my daughter back. I want her home again, to tell her how sorry I am for letting her down. Since her father walked out on us over ten years ago, all I've wanted to do is make up for the disappointment and anguish she felt when he departed and, in doing so, I've done the exact opposite. I've neglected her, not been there for her, when she needed me the most."

"All is not lost, you can rebuild the relationship you once had with your daughter after we've found her."

"And when is that likely to be?"

"We're not sure. We're going to do our best to find her as soon as we can, but we're going to need your help and that of the other parents."

She sighed. "But I don't even know who my daughter's friends are any more. She's stopped talking to me, or rather, I've stopped listening to her. God, could this be classed as child abuse? Will you be reporting me to Social Services for ignoring my duties as a mother?"

"No, that thought hadn't even crossed my mind. Do you have any family in the area who she can turn to for help?"

"No, not really. I have a sister, but we haven't spoken to each other since my husband walked out on me."

Sara inclined her head. "May I ask why?"

"She fancied him. He could never do anything wrong in her eyes, and she blamed me for our marriage failing. I kept our private lives as that, private. She didn't have a clue what he was truly like. He had a different woman on the go every week; maybe that's a slight exaggeration."

"Why didn't you tell her?"

"There's no way she would have believed me. The sun and everything else shone out of his arse, and no, I'm definitely not exaggerating by telling you that. She lost countless boyfriends due to her infatuation with Ian."

"How did Leona feel about the breakup?"

"I think she handled it well. Ian treated us both abysmally come the end. That's the reason I decided enough was enough and ordered him to pack his bags."

"And Leona was okay about it?"

"At first, yes. But as the years passed, she began asking a lot of questions about her father. You have to remember she was only five when he left."

"Has he been in touch with you recently?"

"He's never once contacted us. Not at Christmas or on Leona's birthday. Believe me when I say this, he's an utter bastard and a complete waste of space. I often sit at my desk, when I have a spare minute or two, and wonder what I ever saw in a man who had caused me so much grief over the years."

"Sorry to hear that. Can you think of anyone else Leona might turn to?"

"No. She's close to her friends at school, but I can't for the life of me remember any of their names. I know that makes me sound like a terrible mother and I wouldn't blame you for thinking that either."

"It doesn't. I can see that you've only had her best interests at heart, trying to do what's right for your daughter over the years without her father being around."

"And I've made such a hash of it without even realising it. Will you put out an alert for her? Be airing another conference to announce she's gone missing?"

"If the need arises regarding the conference; an alert has already been actioned. I'm going to leave you my card. If you think of anything that you believe might help our investigation, please get in touch with me straight away."

"I will. I'm sorry we got off on the wrong foot. I hope you can forgive me."

"Forgive and forget, that's my motto. If I were you, I would have my phone next to me all day, even during your meetings, just in case Leona has second thoughts and tries to contact you."

"I'll do that, don't worry. It's time I started putting my daughter first instead of last in my list of priorities."

"Glad to hear it. I'll be in touch the minute we hear anything."

"I can't thank you enough. I hope you have some good news for me soon."

"I hope so, too, it's been a frustrating week for me and my team."

They left the hospital. Once they were outside, Carla did something somewhat random and hugged Sara.

Pulling back, Sara frowned and asked, "What was that for?"

"For being you. You're not praised enough for the work you do. I'm in awe of you most days."

"Get away with you. I did my job, end of."

"No, that woman was ready to deck you the minute we

stepped into that room, but you talked her around and, in the end, had her eating out of your hand."

"Did I heck? I was prepared to be tough on her. As it turned out, she crumbled, probably finding the guilt too much to cope with."

"It doesn't matter. In my opinion you handled it perfectly."

"Enough with the praise..." Sara's mobile rang. She glanced at the caller ID, and the panic rose up from her toes. "Mark, are you all right?"

"I am, Mum's not. I'm going up there, Sara, she's in a coma again."

"Oh no, that's dreadful news. Do you want me to come with you?" She felt the need to ask, despite desperately wanting to remain in Hereford to see the case through to its conclusion.

"No. I'll give you a call if she gets any worse. I should have realised something was wrong when she started having bad headaches."

"You weren't to know, love. Are you sure you don't want me to come with you?"

"I'll be fine. I've put a note on the door. If I get a chance over the weekend, I'll postpone my clients for next week. I suppose it depends on what the doctors say when I get there."

"She's in the best place, Mark. They can monitor her better in the hospital."

"I know. Maybe they shouldn't have released her last month."

"How's your father doing?"

"He's cut up. Scared shitless. Sorry, it's not like me to swear. I need to get home and pack a bag. I want to get on the road before the traffic mounts up on the motorway."

"Okay, will you ring me when you get there?"

"That goes without saying. Sorry to run out on you like this."

"You're not, your parents need you. I can be there within a couple of hours, just call me if things change."

"I will. Love you."

"Love you, too, and take care of yourself as well. I don't have to remind you that you're not long out of hospital yourself, do I?"

"No, I'm good. I promise. I'll call you later."

She blew him a kiss and hung up.

"Did I hear right? Mark's mum is in a coma again?" Carla's concerned expression matched her own.

"I've got a bad feeling about this. She's been struggling since she got out of the hospital."

"Sara, if you believe this is… the end, you should go with him. Sod the case, I can handle things from here. Not as well as you would, granted, but if the kids are all safe and they've been playing silly buggers all this time, then you should pass the baton on and go with Mark."

Sara shook her head. "I can't. I don't want to crowd him, be in the way. He's not been himself recently, and I'd rather not go against his wishes."

"You're kidding me. You never said you had trouble at home. That's typical of you, lending me a shoulder to cry on over my woes, even though you've got problems of your own. You're incredible."

"I'm not, I'm just me. Come on, let's get back to the station. Actually, I might stop off somewhere and have a decent cup of coffee. Are you up for that?"

"Always. Are you sure you're okay?"

"Stop asking, I'm fine."

Sara drew up in Tesco's car park, and they headed for the café they had discovered a few months before. "Do you want anything to eat? It's almost twelve."

"Maybe a cake."

"Yeah, I don't fancy much either. You'd better choose what you want."

Sara had her eye on a fruit scone. She ordered two white coffees and the scone and asked Carla what she wanted.

"I'll have a chocolate éclair, thanks."

They made their way through the café to the table at the rear.

Sara's phone rang as soon as they sat down. "DI Sara Ramsey."

"Sorry to trouble you, boss, it's Barry."

"You're not. Carla and I should be back at the station within half an hour, if it can wait, Barry."

"I don't think it can."

"Let me have it then."

"We've had an alert that Sophie's phone has been turned back on."

"What? That's great news. Where?"

"In the centre of Hereford. She's just used an ATM to withdraw money."

"Shit, okay, we're really close. Which one?"

"Lloyds bank."

"We're on it. Try and get her movements on any CCTV cameras in the area. Do we know if she's on foot?"

"Not sure, boss. We're going over the footage now."

"You're always on the ball. Great job, Barry. We'll keep in touch."

Sara shot out of her chair. "We've got to go, I'm sorry," she apologised to the waitress who was on her way to the table with their drinks and cakes.

"I can quickly put the cakes in a bag. You've paid for them already."

"Thanks, that'd be great. Carla, you grab the cakes, I need to get to the main street, see if I can see her."

"I've got this."

Sara tore out of the door and sprinted up the passageway to the main shopping area. It was market day, so the centre square was chocka with shoppers. Her gaze was drawn to the young woman standing outside Lloyds using the ATM.

Carla caught up with her. Out of breath, she asked, "Have you spotted her yet?"

Sara pointed at the young woman outside the bank.

"Crap, what are we going to do?" Carla asked. "Grab her or keep quiet and follow her?"

"The former, I've had enough of this shit." Sara bolted towards the bank and tapped the young woman on the back, startling her.

"I'm going as quickly as I can, the machine keeps rejecting my card, please be patient," she threw over her shoulder, without turning around.

"Sophie Todd, please face me."

The young woman spun on her heels to look at Sara. "Who? That's not my name."

Shocked to see the woman wasn't who they were searching for, Sara scanned the surrounding area and mumbled an apology.

They moved away from the bank and stepped back when a teenager on a bike rode past them, missing them by inches. "Dumb cops, can't even see what's under your noses." The cyclist laughed and pedalled faster to get away from them as if her feet were on fire.

"Shit! That was her, wasn't it?" Carla asked excitedly.

"It was. She's effing toyed with us long enough. I'm going to have pleasure wiping that smug smile off her face. Come on, are you up for a run?"

Carla gulped. She dipped her head to stare at the three-inch heels she was wearing.

"Bugger, what did I tell you about that yesterday?" Sara

flung her the car keys. "Get back to the car. We need to follow her, any which way we can. I'll call for backup."

"I'm right behind you, I promise."

Sara was thankful she'd chosen her most comfortable ankle boots to work that morning. She upped her pace, but monitored it, not wishing to burn herself out too quickly. She saw the bike just up ahead, travelling down the lane towards Tesco. The last thing she wanted was to alert Sophie she was on her tail, so Sara hid behind the other shoppers where possible. She noticed Sophie casting a glance over her shoulder now and again.

Sara fished her mobile out of her pocket and rang the station. "Jill, is that you?"

"Yes, boss. Oh God, is everything all right? You sound stressed."

"Yes, I'm running after the suspect. I need two teams down here right away. Sophie is on a bicycle. I don't want her getting away from us. We're down near Tesco. Get the teams to join us down here, and I'll give them further instructions when they arrive."

"On it now, boss. Is Carla with you?"

"Yes, she's on her way back to the car. I want to stick with Sophie for as long as I can. She has no idea I'm following her on foot."

"Gotcha. I'll organise the teams now. Good luck."

Sara ended the call and thrust her phone into her pocket again, then she overtook the group of shoppers she'd been close behind. Sophie's speed had appeared to drop to a leisurely pace now.

Maybe she thought two old coppers wouldn't be able to keep up with her. I'll show you, Miss Todd!

Sara was aware that the main roundabout in and out of the city, which split the traffic in various directions, was just around the corner. It would be ideal if she caught the girl before she reached the roundabout, thwarting her escape, but she knew the odds on doing that were slim. Sara made a swift detour through the supermarket car park to the bus terminal at the end. There, she had the perfect view of Sophie when she stopped at the roundabout.

Sara waited for the teenager to make her move; she took the A438 towards Hay-on-Wye. Sara ran back to where the car was parked and saw Carla coming towards her, still holding the cakes. "What kept you?"

"I'm doing my best in these shoes. Maybe I'll listen to your advice in the future."

Carla zapped the fob, and the car doors unlocked. Inside, she handed Sara the key and tried to control her breathing. "I'm desperately unfit. How did that happen?"

"When's your next medical?"

"Don't ask, it's next month. Where are we going now?"

"We'll follow her, at a distance."

"Makes sense."

Sara exited the car park. Unfortunately, the junction was notoriously hard to get out of, giving priority to the motorists travelling on the main road. Once the lights turned to green, she overtook the two cars holding her up and arrived at the huge roundabout, only to get caught up by another set of traffic lights. "Shit, is it just me, or are these lights taking a frigging eternity to change?"

"Calm down. They'll change soon. How many are joining us?"

"I requested the attendance of two teams. I'm hoping they'll understand I meant four people, the same as we had the other day."

"Maybe you should have been more precise with your instructions."

"Possibly, but I was multi-tasking at the time, running

and trying to hide from Sophie whilst still doing my best to keep up with her. No mean feat."

"I'll let you off. Go, the lights are changing."

"What would I do without you here beside me to point out the obvious?"

Carla chuckled and mumbled an apology.

"The teams should be on the road by now, can you check for me?"

Carla picked up the radio. "Car eight, are you there?"

"We're here, Carla. And car seven is right behind me," Craig replied.

"What's your location?"

"We've left the station. We're approaching the large roundabout now."

"That's great. Take the A438 to Hay-on-Wye. We've lost sight of the suspect for now but we're hoping that will change soon."

The radio clicked twice to let them know that Craig had understood.

"Did I do the right thing, calling her a suspect?"

Sara shrugged. "I understood who you meant. I'd say that was a pretty accurate description if she's on the run and trying to evade capture."

"Exactly. Hang on, I think I saw her going around the corner up ahead."

"How far?"

"I'd say about eight or nine cars ahead of us."

"Okay, that's perfect, the last thing we want is her clocking us following her."

"I agree."

A few of the cars turned off at Credenhill, but Sophie continued towards Sugwas Pool. By this time, the rest of the team had caught up and were right behind her.

"I'm sensing a bit of déjà vu here."

"How strange, yes, our last case ended up with us chasing the suspects out this way, too, except they were in a van."

"Yeah, you'd think someone on a bike would be easier to catch, wouldn't you? I've got my doubts whether that'll be the case with Sophie. She's been meticulous with her planning thus far."

"That's true. What about giving her father a call?"

"No frigging way am I doing that, not until we know more about where she's heading. Can you imagine what he'd be like if we lost her? The air would probably turn blue. Nope, I'm going to refrain from telling him until we've caught her. I want to see the look on his face when we reveal the truth about the teenagers' disappearances."

"You mean you're dying to knock him down a peg or two."

"Maybe. Is that childish of me?"

Carla laughed. "If those words had come out of someone else's mouth, I would have said yes, too bloody right. However, knowing what that bloke has put you through this week, I'd say you're well within your rights to keep the truth from him until the very end."

"Let's be fair, it's still an assumption at this stage, anyway."

Carla sat forward and peered out of the windscreen. "Wait, she's turning off. No hand signal to indicate her intentions."

A couple of cars in front tooted their horns at the teenager, and Sophie gave them a V-sign.

Sara bashed the heel of her hand on the steering wheel again as she approached the turnoff which ended up being a cycle track, barely wide enough for a bike, let alone a car. Sara indicated and slammed on her brakes. Craig and Barry did the same in their respective cars behind her. The team got out of the cars.

"Does anyone know where this leads to?"

191

They all shook their heads. "I used to cycle around here when I was in my teens, but this route is new to me," Craig replied.

Sara brought up a map of local cycle routes on her phone. It took a while to load because of the bad reception out in the countryside. "Shit, technology sucks unless you live in the centre of town." After several minutes of waiting for the connection to improve and searching the small screen for the correct route, she sighed and announced, "I don't believe it, it must be so new it's not even been registered on the map yet. Someone up there is showing His might, working against us. What do we do now?"

"Get a drone in the air?" Craig was super quick with his response, and he already had his phone in his hand ready to make the call.

"Yes, do it. It's not like we have any other options available to us."

Sara contemplated their next move until Craig finished his call. "I think we should search the area, just in case she came out further up. Maybe the route joins the main road again a couple of miles up ahead. We'll report back here in half an hour."

The team all raced back to their vehicles, and Sara led the way. The other two cars branched off to search the nearby lanes located around the next couple of bends. Every now and again, Sara would get overwhelmed by regret after allowing the teenager to escape their grasp and let out a mini scream of frustration.

"Jesus, will you please stop making me jump like that? What's done is done, Sara, there's no point in punishing yourself, it's not as if it's going to get us very far."

"I was within touching distance of her, and I let her slip through my fingers, not once but twice. That's unacceptable."

"She's a crafty cow, if what Zoya said about her is true.

So, stop with the self-recrimination. We'll catch her soon, we have to."

"Get in touch with Craig, see what's happening about the drone."

Carla radioed her colleague, and when the response came in, it ticked Sara off even more. The drone had been in the repair shop all week.

"Damn, shit and blast. That's all we need. We'd better get back, meet up with the others and rethink what we need to do next." She carried out a three-point turn in the road and drove back to the rendezvous point as an idea started brewing.

The rest of the team were already there, waiting. Again, the six of them stepped out of the vehicles to have a conflab.

It was then that Sara revealed what she'd been deliberating on the journey back. "If you guys have nothing else to offer, I believe there's only one thing left for us to do."

"What's that?" Carla grimaced.

"I'm going to have to give Mr Todd a call, make him aware of the situation."

"Shit, rather you than me," Carla replied. "He's going to hit the roof when he finds out we've lost her."

"Not if I word it properly, at least, that's what I'm hoping. Sit in your cars, I need to do this in private, guard my words and my reactions. I can't do that while I've got an audience."

Carla inclined her head. "Does that include me?"

"If you don't mind. I won't be long." Sara walked back to her car, her legs trembling beneath her at the thought of speaking with the man she'd had a temperamental relationship with over the past week.

Sara inhaled and exhaled a couple of times and then slipped into her car to make the call. "Hello, Mr Todd. Is it convenient to have a chat with you? Sorry, it's Inspector

Ramsey calling." She punched herself in the thigh for the lack of confidence she'd caught in her tone.

"It is, Inspector. Do you have any news for me?"

"Possibly. We've received reports of a possible sighting of Sophie."

"My God, where? Is she okay? Was she with anyone else or by herself? What are you doing to find her?"

The questions came thick and fast, something that Sara had expected. Her head was spinning. She thrust her shoulders back and said, "If you'll let me finish?"

"Answer my damn questions, at least the main ones. Where, and is she okay?"

"She appears to have been. She was seen out near Sugwas Pool."

"What?"

There was something in his tone that Sara instantly detected. "Do you know anyone who lives out that way, sir?"

"I did. My sister. Her house is for sale. I'm in charge of selling it."

"Interesting. Do you have a key to the property?"

"Of course I do. Wait, what are you getting at? Are you telling me you believe the kidnapper is holding her hostage at the house?"

"Possibly. Is there any chance that Sophie might have got her hands on the key?"

"Gosh, yes, it's possible. I can check the key cupboard in the hallway. I'm working from home today. Hold the line, will you?"

"I will." Her heart raced, and bile burnt the back of her throat with the anticipation as she waited for him to return.

"It's missing. I swear it was there at the weekend. What does it mean? That the kidnappers broke into the house, stole the key along with my daughter? Did Sophie tell them about the house?"

"Maybe. Can you give me the address?"

"No, I'm going out there myself."

"No, I can't allow you to do that, Mr Todd. You must leave this to me to handle. These people could be armed and dangerous." Every time he spoke, she closed her eyes, fearing that he would insist on being there, possibly getting in their way.

"This is so frustrating for me. All I want to do is see my daughter again and..."

"Please, trust me. Can I have the address, please?" Sara insisted.

"This is against my better judgement, Inspector. It's number twelve Park Road, Canon Bridge. Would it be all right if I met you there?"

Sara thought there would be a backlash from him if she refused and, as she and her team were much closer to the property than he was, she found herself agreeing to his proposition. "Okay, only if you promise not to interfere."

"You have my word. Are you at the station?"

"Yes," she lied. "My team and I are just heading out that way now."

"I'll see you there."

"Look forward to it."

He was the one to end the call. Sara could imagine him tearing out of the house and jumping into his fast car, breaking the speed limit to get to the address before them.

Sara shot out of the car and shared the news with the others. "I had to agree to Todd joining us at the address, so we'd better get over there now. I bought us some time by telling him we were setting off from the station. Let's hit the road, folks."

Carla joined her, and they sped off. The two other cars followed them in a mini convoy. Ten minutes later, Sara drew up at the end of the road. With Sophie spotting her in

195

the city centre earlier, she decided to send Craig and Barry ahead of them, on foot, to check out the property.

"Just pretend you're having an innocent conversation as you pass. Casually check out the front of the house, see if the curtains are closed or open and if there's any sign of movement inside the property. Make it snappy, though, there's no telling how long Todd is going to take to get here."

They both nodded and started a conversation about football as they walked towards the house. Marissa and Christine jumped in the back seat of Sara's car, and the four of them watched the proceedings with a mixture of interest and anticipation.

"Maybe a couple of us should have kept an eye on the back of the property. There's an alley over there." Carla pointed out the opening not twenty yards from them.

"Good call. Take Marissa with you, Carla. I don't have to tell you what to do, just ensure you're not seen."

"Are you ready, Marissa?" Carla peered over her shoulder.

Marissa replied by getting out of the car and joining Carla by the bonnet.

"I hope we're doing the right thing here," Sara mumbled to Christine.

"Believe in them, boss, they won't screw it up."

Sara watched on, her head swivelling from in front of her to the left where the entrance to the alley was as her team moved closer to the house. "Christine, can you keep an eye behind us for Todd, he's bound to arrive soon."

"On it. You sound worried."

"I'm anxious. There's no telling how these kids are going to react or what the hell is going on inside that house."

"If it's any consolation, it's a semi-detached place. I suppose if the kids had been rowdy, we would have had a complaint registered at the station by now from the neighbours."

"You're right, unless the neighbours are away. That might be why no one has called the police to tell us a bunch of kids have moved in. There's no For Sale sign outside the house either."

"I wonder if Sophie took it off the market without her father knowing."

"Possibly. I wouldn't put it past the little minx. The boys are on their way back."

"All clear behind us," Christine informed her.

Sara's gaze drifted left when Carla and Marissa exited the alley and jogged back to the car. The ladies got in the car before Craig and Barry reached them.

"Lots of mess in the back garden, lager and pop cans on the patio. The back door is open; we're going to need to be aware of that when we make our move."

Sara nodded, her mind whirling. She opened her car door as Craig and Barry arrived. They crouched beside Sara, the door shielding them from view in case anyone at the house was watching them.

"How did you get on?"

"The curtains were open when we walked past but closed on the way back," Barry said. "I saw two girls and a boy in the front room. The girl, I'm presuming it was Sophie, looked pretty worked up, gesticulating and shouting at the others."

"Seems to be getting a bit heated in there. Carla and Marissa checked the back; the door is open. I'm thinking we should go in that way. It seems too good an opportunity to miss. Christine, why don't you and Craig take the front? Knock on the door to distract them. In the meantime, the rest of us will go through the back way, try to catch them unaware."

"Sounds good to me." Christine opened her door.

"Give us a few minutes to get into position first. Let's do this. Remember, they may only be a group of teenagers, but they've got their heads screwed on, they must have, to have come up with such an audacious plan."

The rest of them agreed.

"Okay, let's get in there quickly. I'm conscious of the time restraint we're under with Todd on his way."

Christine and Craig got into position, ready to walk back to the front of the property while Sara and her other three colleagues left the car and dived up the alley.

"I want to get in there promptly, no noise, let's surprise them. Got that?"

Barry raised his thumb while Carla and Marissa both nodded.

They made their way up the alley, aware that their colleagues would be approaching the front door at the same time. Sara eased the back gate open, took in her surroundings and motioned for her colleagues to enter the house behind her. A girl shouted in a room at the front of the house, and the other two occupants were trying to calm her down.

Sara's heart pounded, and her breathing increased with every step she took. She paused in the hallway. At the front door she saw the outlines of Christine and Craig. The bell rang, which made the girl shout even more.

"I told you they were on to us. You should have kept the curtains closed. Why the fuck did you open them?"

"Will you keep the noise down?" the boy responded. "We'll just ignore them; they'll take the hint and go away."

"Will they? You dumb shit, they're coppers, they never give up. I'm out of here. I'll go out the back way."

Sara stood tall with Barry beside her, blocking the hallway.

The other two teenagers both tried to reason with Sophie. She was having none of it and appeared in the hall-way. She screamed, not expecting to see Sara and her team

198

already inside the house. Sophie ran back into the lounge and shut the door, or tried to. Barry was alert and quick to act. He shoulder-charged it to prevent the kids from barricading themselves inside. Sara followed Barry into the room, and Carla let their colleagues in. The lounge was quite large but seemed small with the number of people now filling it.

Sara produced her ID. "I'm DI Sara Ramsey, the SIO, Senior Officer in charge of the investigation. We know what you've been up to, Sophie, Daniel and Leona. Your little game of attempting to make your parents sit up and take notice of you has worked, but I fear it has also backfired at the same time."

"Typical of a copper to say that," Sophie barked at her. "That's bullshit, you didn't have a clue what was going on. All this was my plan, to teach our parents a lesson they wouldn't forget."

"I know exactly what your plan was and of your intention to have people think that you'd been kidnapped. Maybe you've forgotten the key to having a relationship with your parents, the art of communication. Having spoken to all of them over the past week, I have to inform you that each and every one of them admit they're guilty of working long hours. The reasons? To give you the best lives possible. I don't think you realise how difficult it is to raise a child, or should I say teenager, when you're a single parent. They work extra hours to make your lives better. Granted, it probably doesn't seem that way to you, but I assure you, your welfare has always been the driving force behind them putting in their long days."

"Screw that, we don't want the 'best things in life'," Sophie whined. "All I've ever wanted is for my dad to sit down and be with me after school, to help me with my homework if I have a query about it. He's never there. Not when I need him the most. He works six days a week. I'm stuck in the house on Saturdays as well, while he's out, seeing to people in our community. He's got no time for me and what I want. No time to service my needs in this world, only the needs of those in his constituency. I come at the very bottom of the list."

"You're wrong, Sophie. He's been extremely worried about you this week. Did you see the press conference? The heartfelt appeal he put out?"

"I did. It was all staged."

"It was not. Far from it. I didn't arrange it, he did. Conferences of that size take hours to sort out. He did that, off his own bat. In all honesty, I was furious with him at the time because he went above my head, but it was his love for you that drove him to put out that conference the day after you went missing. You're going to need to take my word on this, but in all my years on the Force, no father has ever gone above and beyond the way he has for you."

There was a sudden burst of applause from behind Sara. She turned to see Ray Todd sheepishly standing in the doorway.

"The inspector is right, Sophie, you may not realise what you mean to me, but every hour of my working day is spent worrying about you and doing what's right for you."

Sophie shook her head. "I don't believe you. You're just saying it because you believe it's the right thing to say in front of an audience." Tears emerged, in spite of her angry words.

Todd passed Sara and her team and closed the distance between him and his daughter. He held out his arms. Sara could tell Sophie was on the brink of giving in but then saw a sudden change in her, and the teenager ended up backing away from him.

"Don't think you can wrap me around your little finger,

Dad, it won't wash. You don't care about me. The minute Mum died, I knew our lives would change forever."

"Of course they'd change. I've always tried to do my best for you, Sophie. You've wanted for nothing over the years."

"I wanted your *time*. I *needed* you to stop working for five minutes when you're at home and pay *me* some attention. I don't think that's too much to ask, do you? Ten years Mum has been gone. Yes, Auntie Kerry was there for me, but then we buried her, and the loss was immense all over again, and where were you? At work. You're always *at work*. You didn't take time off to grieve for her. You never asked me how I felt after she'd passed. She was like a second mother to me, and then I was robbed of her love and compassion. Can you imagine what impact that had on me? I'll answer for you, no, you couldn't imagine because you didn't want to."

He shook his head, and his eyes watered, matching his daughter's obvious signs of emotion. "You're wrong, I coped with her loss the only way I knew how to, by throwing myself into my work. I regret that now, after hearing all of this, but at the time, I genuinely thought it was the right thing to do, for both our sakes."

"Why? Because showing any kind of emotion is wrong in your eyes? Deemed to be a weakness to a man of your stature in the community? You're my father, that should come first, top the list of your priorities. I was forced to grieve on my own. If it hadn't been for Auntie Kerry... it doesn't matter, you don't care anyway."

Todd tried to take a step towards Sophie.

She raised her hand to stop him. "No, I don't want you anywhere near me. It's taken me and my friends to pull off this plan, to make you sit up and take notice of me. How long did it take you to realise I'd be here? It should have been your first consideration, not your last."

"I'm at fault, for all of it, Soph. I should have told the

inspector about this house, however, why would I if I suspected you'd been abducted? Think about it, it makes sense. Daniel's and Leona's mothers both thought the same as me, we believed someone had abducted you, and for all we knew, you were on your way out of the country in the back of a lorry, being smuggled by people traffickers. I bet you hadn't thought about that scenario, had you, when you devised this plan to punish us, am I right?"

Sophie's head dropped, and the shame descended.

"He's right, Soph. None of this is right, us disappearing like this," Leona jumped in. "We've made our point, it's time for us to make amends with our parents, give them a chance to right their wrongs. If they were at fault in the first place."

"I agree. I need to go home, I feel bad for putting my mother through this pain and torment, just so she would take notice of me. As much as I love you guys, I realise now, all of this has been a huge mistake. It's time for us to go home, to beg for forgiveness from the people who love us the most," Daniel said. He glanced at Sara and smiled weakly at her. "I want to go home, to be with my mum."

Sara patted him on the shoulder. "You'll get your wish. Go with Christine, she'll call your mother, ask her to pick you up from the station."

"Thank you. I'm sorry for the trouble I've caused. It seemed a good idea at the time."

Sara smiled and placed her hand under his chin, forcing him to look at her. "Apology accepted. This time it turned out for the best… when you get home, I need you to have an open and frank conversation with your mother. Will you promise me you'll do that, Daniel?"

"I promise. If she's willing to meet me halfway then I think things will turn out to be very different."

"I want you to think of this as a learning curve going

forward in life. If we don't converse with people, they won't know what our needs and desires are."

"I'll take that on board, thank you."

Christine led Daniel out of the house.

"Leona, how do you feel about this situation?" Sara asked.

"I'll be glad to go home. I just hope Mum can find it in her heart to forgive me."

"That goes without saying. Go with Marissa, she'll take you back to the car and you can speak to your mother from there."

"Thank you. I'm sorry, too, because we caused you so much trouble."

Sara smiled. "You're all right, all of you, that's a huge relief, not only to your parents but to me and my team as well. Take care of yourself, and your mother does love you, whether you struggle to believe that at times or not."

"I know. Thank you. Maybe the three of us could meet up a few times a week, be there for each other when one of our parents is working late."

Sara nodded, pleased to hear the teenager come up with an alternative plan. "That's an excellent idea and something you need to work out with your parents. Take care."

Leona, clearly embarrassed, smiled, linked hands with Marissa and left the house.

"That just leaves you two," Sara said, her glance shifting between Sophie and her father who had mellowed considerably in her opinion, since she'd first met him at the beginning of the week. "Now, are you two going to make up or do I have to bash your heads together?"

Ray held out his arms. It took a while for Sophie to bow to the pressure, a gamut of emotions fleetingly crossing her face. Eventually, she let out a huge sigh and walked into her father's arms. Sara stroked the girl's back and smiled at her father. He winked at her and mouthed that he would be in touch soon.

Sara and the rest of the team left the house via the front door this time, which was much more civilised. She high-fived each of them. "Well done, team, another successful case under our belts. I appreciate all your efforts; it has been a hellishly frustrating week for all of us."

"It has, but we made it through to the end," Carla agreed. She peered at her watch. "You should get your arse on the road, leave all the paperwork for us to sort out. Mark and his family need you."

"Are you sure? I'd prefer to be with him, even if he doesn't want me there. Can you catch a lift back with the others?"

"There you go again, worrying about everyone else. Go, and yes, that's an order."

Sara hugged her partner and ran back to the car.

"Ring me later," Carla shouted after her.

"You've got it."

EPILOGUE

As it happened, Sara arrived at Mark's parents' house half an hour after he did. He was shocked and relieved to see her standing on the doorstep when he opened the front door.

"What the...? God, I'm so pleased to see you. How did you manage to get away?"

"We wrapped up the case earlier than anticipated. All three teenagers are now home safe with their parents. Enough about work, how is your father doing and, more importantly, how's your mum?"

"Well, I'm glad you're here. Dad will be, too. He's getting ready. The consultant has asked us to join him at the hospital. Do you want to come?"

"Silly question. Of course I do." She touched his cheek, and he leaned into the palm of her hand. "How are you holding up?"

"Ask me later. I'm running on adrenaline right now, ensuring Dad's all right." He lowered his voice and added, "He was a mess when I got here. I've reassured him enough to make sure he knows she's in the right place. I'm sorry, there's no time for us to have a drink."

She waved away his concerns and kissed him on the lips. "Stop worrying about me. I'll grab a coffee at the hospital if the consultant keeps us waiting."

He led her into the lounge.

Mark's father entered the room a few minutes later and was surprised to see Sara standing next to his son. "Oh, Sara... you'll never know how much it means to me having you here with us."

She took a step forward and hugged him. "I'm glad I could make it. How are you, James?"

"I'm fine. My darling Liz isn't, though. We need to get a move on. Will you come with us?"

"I'd love to. I'll drive."

Mark kissed her on the top of the head. "Thank you."

SARA DROVE to the hospital with Mark and his father giving her directions at the appropriate times. They raced through the corridors, a few minutes late for their scheduled meeting with the consultant. He was waiting for them outside Liz's private room.

His expression was unreadable as they approached. Sara's stomach rolled over several times. She gripped Mark's hand for support. He squeezed it tighter the closer they got to Mr Gallagher.

"We're sorry we're late, the traffic was bad at this time of night," Mark spluttered the apology.

Mr Gallagher held up his hand. "There's no need to apologise, you're here now."

"How is she, Doctor?" Sara asked.

"Maybe Mr Fisher would prefer to take a seat." Mr Gallagher pointed at a chair just behind him, and James sank into it. "It's never easy sharing this kind of news with a patient's family."

Sara closed her eyes, fearing the worst. Mark clung to her arm as well as her hand.

"How bad is she, Doctor?" Sara felt the need to take over.

"As bad as it can get, I'm afraid. We have run all the tests and found several tumours in Mrs Fisher's brain. I regret to tell you that she only has a few days left to live."

Sara's world stopped. Her gaze drifted to Mark's father, whose mouth had dropped open, and then she glanced up at Mark who looked stunned by the news.

"Can we see her?" Sara asked.

"By all means."

He showed them into the room, and Sara couldn't help but gasp. Mrs Fisher was unconscious, her head bandaged and her complexion sallow.

I have to suck it up, support Mark and his father. This isn't about me, it's about them.

Mr Gallagher left the room.

Mark hugged his father and encouraged him to sit next to his mother and hold her hand. "Talk to her, Dad."

"I can't. I don't know what to say."

The three of them sat in silence by Liz's bed for the next eighteen hours until she took her last breath and slipped away.

"Don't leave me, Liz. Come back, life won't be worth living if you go," James said, his voice full of emotion and catching in his throat. His hand shook as he reached for Liz's to hold one final time.

Sara found the scene both touching and heartbreaking. She sobbed and clung to her husband who had been rendered speechless, tears streaming down his colourless cheeks.

They all stared on in silence at Liz's lifeless body and Sara was left wondering what life would have in store for them all in the future with Liz no longer around.

THE END

THANK YOU FOR READING GONE... But Where?, Sara and Carla's next adventure can be found here Last Man Standing

HAVE you read any of my fast paced other crime thrillers yet? Why not try the first book in the award-winning Justice series Cruel Justice here.

OR THE FIRST book in the spin-off Justice Again series, Gone In Seconds.

WHY NOT TRY the first book in the DI Sam Cobbs series, set in the beautiful Lake District, To Die For.

PERHAPS YOU'D PREFER to try one of my other police procedural series, the DI Kayli Bright series which begins with The Missing Children.

OR MAYBE YOU'D enjoy the DI Sally Parker series set in Norfolk, Wrong Place.

. . .

OR MY GRITTY police procedural starring DI Nelson set in Manchester, <u>Torn Apart.</u>

OR MAYBE YOU'D like to try one of my successful psychological thrillers <u>She's Gone</u>, <u>I KNOW THE TRUTH</u> or <u>Shattered Lives.</u>

KEEP IN TOUCH WITH M A COMLEY

Pick up a FREE novella by signing up to my newsletter today.
https://BookHip.com/WBRTGW

BookBub
www.bookbub.com/authors/m-a-comley

Blog

http://melcomley.blogspot.com

Why not join my special Facebook group to take part in monthly giveaways.

Readers' Group

Printed in Dunstable, United Kingdom